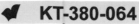

I would like to thank Mark Ashdown and his siblings for the valuable insight into their father's service during World War Two. I'd also like to thank Tony Bradman and the team at Scholastic for asking me to take part in this wonderful and much-needed series. Bali Rai

While the events described and some of the characters in this book may be based on actual historical events and real people, Fazal Khan is a fictional character, created by the author, and his story is a work of fiction.

Scholastic Children's Books,
Euston House, 24 Eversholt Street,
London NW1 1DB, UK

A division of Scholastic Ltd
London ~ New York ~ Toronto ~ Sydney ~ Auckland
Mexico City ~ New Delhi ~ Hong Kong

First published in the UK by Scholastic Ltd, 2019

ISBN 978 1407 19136 2

Printed and bound by
CPI Group (UK) Ltd, Croydon, CR0 4YY

2 4 6 8 10 9 7 5 3 1

www.scholastic.co.uk

NOW OR NEVER

BALI RAI

Series Consultant:
Tony Bradman

◾SCHOLASTIC

PROLOGUE

It was still dark when I left my village, carrying only what I needed to travel. My family were fast asleep, and I did not wake them. I was running away, desperate to find my fortune, desperate to follow in my grandfather's footsteps. My decision was swift, but the planning took some months. Now, I was finally ready to leave. And even though my heart ached at the thought of my mother's distress and the tears of my younger sisters, I did not waver. My grandfather had taught me to believe in myself, and to be sure in my actions. Now that I was going, and he was no longer with me, I wondered what he might think. Whether he was looking down on me as I sneaked away.

I stopped a mile from the village, which would soon be consumed by the city of Rawalpindi and become another of its many districts. I stood by a grove of trees, under which my grandfather, my *baba*, had often sat.

There, he would take shade from the sun, chatting with his friend Mr Singh, playing cards. There, he taught me many lessons about life and told stories of his time in Europe, fighting in what they had called the Great War.

Now, as I stood and thought of him awhile, I was leaving to have my own adventures, hoping to follow Baba's example and become a man. I had no idea what awaited me, and I will admit to some fear. Mostly, however, I was excited. Baba had no gravestone to mark his passing. Instead, I touched his favourite wooden seat, under his favourite tree, and asked for his blessing.

Then, without another rearward glance, I set off on my journey...

1

We disembarked in 1939, during the coldest winter for a hundred years, many thousands of miles from home. As Company 32, of the Royal Indian Army Service Corps, we had been ordered to Europe alongside three other units. They called us Force K-6 and we were sixteen hundred men and close to two thousand mules strong, with a few horses in addition. Our British rulers had made a terrible mistake when the war began, ignoring animal corps, and relying solely on vehicles for transport. Only, when the British Expeditionary Force reached France, they found themselves bogged down by muddy and then frozen roads and lanes and fields, unable to get supplies to the front lines quickly enough. That became our job.

On our arrival, everything was covered in snow and ice – the houses, the streets, the fields. The locals shivered as they passed us by, hidden under thick layers of clothing, with moth-eaten blankets wrapped around them. The rivers and streams were frozen, and the bows of every tree weighed down by ice and snow. Every scene seemed leeched of colour and joy and warmth, as though the whole country lay under some great depression beyond the war. I came from Rawalpindi, in the far north of India, and was used to the cold, but this was something else. It chilled my bones, and set my teeth chattering. Occasionally, the biting winds even made conversation difficult, so badly did my jaws vibrate. But at least I had a voice to find.

Our mules were silent. Always silent. They had been gagged; their vocal cords surgically altered before we embarked on the long journey from India to Marseille, in France.

"That should stop them alerting the enemy," a fellow soldier had said.

Yet, I could not bring myself to approve of such barbarism. I was very young and had little experience of cruelty. But, when we reached France, I witnessed the horror and savagery of war firsthand. Cruelty lingered everywhere in conflict. A nasty business and no mistake.

When we docked at Marseille, I had grown excited by the prospect of a foreign land. Barely eighteen according to my forged documents, in reality I was just past my fifteenth birthday. I had lied to enlist and run away from home, desperate to emulate my late grandfather, who had fought during the Great War and told tales of bravery and camaraderie, honour and duty. I looked older than my years, but at heart I was still a boy. A boy who wanted to become a man.

I knew my actions would hurt my family and cause them sorrow, but I enlisted regardless. The pull of my dreams was much too strong. I did not even stop to think. Looking back, I was immature and selfish, and yet I felt great pride too. I joined many others from my city, as we trained under the British some distance from my home. We were attached to an animal unit, specifically mules, and taught to care for our charges. To understand our vital role in supplying combat units with ammunition and food, and whatever else they required during battle. In India, we saw little action. Then, very quickly after I enlisted, the call came to join the war in Europe. Soon everything changed.

The French people were not particularly welcoming, but they did not trouble us either. Most were too busy trying to keep warm and too frightened of what lay ahead. The same lack of cordiality was true of our British comrades, which I found harder to take. Surely, we were all brothers in arms, fighting the same fight?

However, it was wartime, and there was no use in dwelling on such things. Besides our Captain, John Ashdown, made sure we were looked after.

"We are here to do a job," he'd tell us. "As important as any other. Remember that."

After disembarking ourselves and our animals, we were sent to a transit camp outside Marseille, and from there we headed north. Soon each company was sent to different postings. We moved around a great deal, becoming skilled in erecting tents at each new camp. Often, we tethered the mules under trees, or tied them to buildings, covering them in blankets as protection from the cold and retreating to our shelters. Despite the freezing temperatures, we tried to warm ourselves with tea and hardtack biscuits, and some tinned bully beef. It was far from ideal, but it was all we had.

During my first month, I was weary and cold, and uncertain of why I'd chosen to join up. I had dreamt of grand buildings, exotic food and friendly folk, but all I saw of that great country was fields and trees and mud and snow. Rawalpindi was chaotic and haphazard, warm and inviting. The France I first encountered was none of these things. My closest comrade, Mushtaq Ahmad, grew annoyed when I said as much aloud.

"What did you think we would find, brother?" Mush asked me. "We are at war."

"I just expected more" I replied.

"*More?*" asked Mush. "We are just Indians. These people do not think of us as equals. This is not *our* war, Faz."

Mush shook his head. He was paler than me, with green eyes and a hooked nose. His jet-black moustache swept around his mouth and was curled at the ends.

"It is our duty, Mush," I replied. "You know this."

We Indian soldiers had a motto, a rallying cry for when things were going awry. If anyone in India questioned our loyalty to the British, we would simply say "*Hukum Hai*" – it is our duty. Now, I reminded Mush of that duty.

"*Duty?*" he replied. "I am here because I had nothing, and the British pay us. I was a peasant farmer at home, without even a field to call my own. My duty is to you and the rest of our brothers. I do not care about kings and empires."

"Look," I added, picking up a tin cup full of tea. "We are cold and tired, and in a foreign land. But we have a task to perform, and inshallah, we will not shirk it. We do not run from hard work."

"I know this," he replied. "But there is nothing more than this, Fazal."

"I just thought. . ." I began

"You thought you might find a nice French girl to

take home?" he joked. "I'm sure we will meet a few blind ones."

"Idiot," I said with a grin.

"Buffoon," he replied.

Eventually I settled into a routine. Upon waking and washing, and after a breakfast of canned meat, hard bread and tea, I would groom the mules alongside my comrades. This involved checking them for signs of illness or infection and brushing their coats. Then we would check their hooves for stones and other detritus, removing anything we found with spiked hoof picks. Occasionally, the veterinary officers would ask about the mules' welfare, and I would be asked to translate.

"You've a good grasp of the language, Khan," Sergeant Buckingham said one morning.

"Yes, sir," I replied. "My school followed a British curriculum."

"You come from a well-to-do family then?" said Sergeant Buckingham.

"Not so well-to-do," I told him. "But we have decent enough lives. My father works as a court administrator and my grandfather fought during the Great War."

"My father too," he replied, his expression darkening. "Died at The Somme. I never really knew him."

"I am sorry," I said. "My condolences."

"It's fine, Private Khan," said Sergeant Buckingham. "Each of us has made sacrifices for the Empire. Now, any problems with the animals?"

"No, sir."

"Good, good," he replied. "Saves me a blasted job. I'm off to get a cup of chai. Carry on!"

As he sauntered away, I saluted and got back to my task. The mules stood with their heads bowed, many of them feeding from cloth bags tied around their necks. My next job was to weigh out a serving of oats for their feed, and I called to Mush.

"Scales," I said.

Mush nodded and brought them across.

"Feeling better today?" I asked.

"Yes, brother," he replied. "*Hukum Hai. . .*"

2

We moved around France until May 1940, before a change of fortune sent us headlong into a nightmare. Captain Ashdown gathered us one morning and broke the news, at a temporary camp in a small town between Lens and Lille.

"It seems that Hitler has decided to invade Belgium," he told us.

Murmurs of anxiety spread through the men, but the Captain hushed them with a cough. He was tall, with a neatly trimmed moustache, and wore spectacles under his peaked hat. His khaki uniform was immaculate, as always, and his black leather boots shone. Captain Ashdown loved my country, was fluent in Punjabi and Urdu, and always respectful of we Indians. It made him all the more admirable

"German troops have marched into Belgium, via The Netherlands and Luxembourg. So, naturally our combat units have been sent to block the enemy advance."

A cheer went up amongst the men, and Captain Ashdown smiled before holding up his right hand.

"However," he added, "the Germans are trying to outflank us. They're advancing through the Ardennes Forest, just north of the Maginot Line."

The man next to me gasped. Mush leant over and whispered.

"I thought this Maginot could not be broken?"

I shrugged.

"That is what they said," I replied.

If the Germans managed to cross the Maginot Line of defence, they would cut us off from Allied troops in the North. That would be catastrophic. Captain Ashdown waited a moment, letting the news sink in.

"Therefore," he said, "and with utmost haste, we must move north. We cannot let the Germans outwit us. We leave in two hours."

As he strode away, the men around me spoke in hushed and fearful tones. So far, we had seen no combat. Sergeant Buckingham had called it the Phoney War, parroting British newspapers. Now the real war was upon us. "Hurry up!" the Sergeant yelled. "You heard the Captain. *Jaldi*!"

I rushed to gather my meagre belongings and then went to help prepare and tether the mules. In the end, I was given three animals to guide, and within the hour, we were ready to march. Two of my mules had dark, nut-brown hides and sturdy hindquarters. The third was slightly smaller, with pale brown hide the colour of my grandfather's eyes, and white patches on its legs. All three had white snouts and the elongated ears of their donkey fathers.

"Perhaps I will call you Baba," I told the smaller mule, using the Punjabi word for granddad. "And, perhaps I can tell you what I cannot tell him?"

The other two raised their heads, as though they understood and were envious.

"I won't forget you either," I said to them. "You can be my sisters, although you do smell better. . ."

I laughed at my own joke and saw Mush shaking his head.

"You utter clown!" He laughed.

All around us, across the makeshift base, every unit was on the move. It seemed as though the entire Allied Force was preparing to leave.

"Will no men stay on here?" I asked Mush.

"Perhaps some French troops," he told me. "Besides, if we cannot stop the Germans, the war will be over by September. And not in our favour."

By the deadline, we were on the move. The combat units had trucks and other vehicles, as did the officers. We muleteers marched in convoy, leading our animals behind us. As we left the makeshift base, scared and angry locals accosted us, many seeming to curse us in French. About a mile north, as we marched through a village, some local women ran towards us. One of them, similar in age to my mother, took hold of my free hand and implored in French. But I had no idea what she was saying, and I simply shook my head.

It felt wrong to be leaving the people undefended, but our need was great and time short. The thought of our troops surrounded by the Germans was too much to bear. We had come to France to win the war, not lose it in the first genuine skirmish. Should the worst happen, the shame and dishonour would haunt us forever. After running away, I could not return to face my family after such humiliation, and nor could my comrades. It was the second harsh lesson that war taught me.

The journey took us through some breathtakingly beautiful scenery. I was much taken by France's forests and rivers and hills and fields. My grandfather had longed to return to the West, but age and illness, and finally death had made that impossible. Now, I wished he were with me. Wished that I could write him a letter, even. Perhaps, I thought, I might compose one anyway, as soon as we find time to rest. It did not matter that he would never read it. Just that I wrote down my thoughts and expressed my feelings.

Only, rest was but a fanciful dream. We did not really rest. We merely stopped and struggled to regain our strength, before leaving again, wearier than ever. We did not even have time to pray, and this upset many of my comrades. It was another sacrifice for King and Empire, and it bothered me greatly.

"Why no trucks for us?" one man asked. "Surely we would move faster that way?"

I shrugged.

"It is our lot," I told him. "Our duty."

"Pah!" he replied. "Forget duty. This is about our worth. We are not important enough."

I turned away, and ignored him, but I could not disregard his words. The further we travelled, and the wearier I became, the more I realised he was correct. To the British, we seemed as worthy as our mules. Not all of the British, of course. Captain Ashdown made sure to check on our welfare throughout the trek, but nonetheless, my feelings remained. And just like my mules, I felt voiceless too.

Soon things grew more serious. We began to encounter panicked French locals and bomb-damaged vehicles, roads and buildings. On two occasions, we passed by dead bodies left to rot in ditches. Rumours of German fighter planes spread amongst us, and we quickly realised how difficult our situation had become. Scores of locals had joined us, carrying what little they could. I saw frail and elderly people being escorted, and mothers carrying babies. The locals fled on pushbikes and horse-drawn carts, and everywhere we went, we began to find burnt-out Allied vehicles and defences.

"We're destroying anything we can't carry," Sergeant Buckingham told me during a brief respite. "We'll be doomed if the Germans attack us with our own weapons."

I was checking Baba's hooves when the Sergeant approached. He looked a little drunk.

"But won't we need weapons to fight back?" I asked.

The Sergeant smirked.

"I'm not sure we *will* fight back," he told me. "Certainly not in the near future. This looks like a retreat, Khan. Hitler's outsmarted the toffs back at home, I'd say. It's a mess, all of this."

Some hours later, we stopped in woodland and drew breath. Baba and my sisters seemed agitated so, despite my desire to sleep, I tried to calm them. If you have never seen a voiceless mule bray, I pray that you never will. Baba turned his head towards me and as he tried to cry out, his head shook, and his jaw snapped open and shut. I rubbed his head and back, and whispered kind words, but he did not calm down. Soon, the others followed, as though I'd entered some nightmare. The sight of them caused me great sadness.

"Mine have done the same thing," Mush told me. "They are agitated and scared, just like us."

I shook my head.

"They cannot speak," I told him. "So, they are less fortunate than us. If I am scared, I can speak to you. We have taken that from these beasts. It is an indignity, brother. It is cruel."

"Like the Empire took from us," said Mush, and I raised an eyebrow.

"But what of duty?" I asked him.

"Duty and honour are not the same things," he replied. "There is no honour in this Empire. Yet, I have sworn upon my own honour to fight, and I will do that. But with my eyes open."

"Eyes open?" I asked, unsure of what he meant.

"Yes, brother," he explained. "I know what I am fighting for, and I am a man of my word. But being honourable does not prevent us from being honest, too.

Truth is a parent of honour."

I sat and took some hardtack from my bag and crunched on it.

"And what is the truth?" I asked Mush.

"Simple," he said. "We are beasts of burden, leading beasts of burden, for King and Empire. We chose this life, even though the Empire thinks so little of us. We took on this duty, and we cannot shirk it."

"So, we must simply endure?" I asked.

"Yes," Mush told me. "We have no other choice. I must survive, for the sake of my wife and children. I cannot fail them."

I thought of my home village, my mother and my family. I thought of the pretty girls who walked down the lanes around my house, the fat mangoes that were so prized in the summer, and the fields of wheat and corn that seemingly stretched on for days, bathed in glorious sunshine. I thought of spiced and fried onions, and thick *dal* with corn *roti*, and the sweet and creamy texture of *rassa malai*, my favourite dessert of curds in sugary milk.

"We had a choice," I eventually said to Mush. "We could have stayed at home."

"*Home?*" he replied. "We are very far from home, brother. Not even these mules, these little ships that carry us forward, can take us home. Until we have served our purpose, this is home."

I sighed and closed my eyes and longed for some real sleep. That when I heard the Stuka's dreadful siren. . .

3

In Rawalpindi, we have hornets the length of a man's middle finger. They are yellow and green, and orange and black, and should they swarm, you would not escape with your life. That is what the German aircraft, the Stukas, came to remind me of, and they were even deadlier.

I heard its engine first, a distant droning sound. But as it drew near, another sound made my legs shake. It was an incessant whining, like Death warning us to take refuge.

"ENEMY PLANE!" I heard Sergeant Buckingham holler. "GET TO COVER!"

I grabbed hold of my animals' reins and led them deeper into the trees. Mules are perfect creatures for war. They are resilient and agile and can go where vehicles cannot. But as they stepped over fallen logs and trudged through thick, brown mud, they seemed to sense the alarm. My lead mule suddenly stopped, causing the others to follow suit.

"Come on, Baba!" I urged, pulling on the rope, but he refused to budge.

"If you do not hide, Baba, we will die," I warned.

The fighter was closing in and its machine guns began to clatter. All around us, the bullets stripped away chunks of bark. My comrades yelled and screamed in panic and hid in the bushes and undergrowth. The mules panicked too, and some of the men tried to calm them. I could not leave my animals alone, so I hid behind them, and awaited my fate.

But the Stuka dropped its bombs closer to the road, and the explosions merely shook the ground beneath me. I heard more screaming, and shouting, and then it was gone, leaving us shocked and deafened, and frightened to our cores. As we gathered ourselves, I saw Captain Ashdown rushing towards us.

"Khan!" he yelled when he spotted me. "Civilian casualties on the road. We need to help them. Now!"

Two of the medics came with me, and when we reached the road, we saw absolute carnage. The bombs had hit a cart and blown a hollow into the road. On either side lay destroyed trucks and jeeps, and human bodies, too. There was nothing to be done for the dead, but many of the wounded were beyond help too. It was more than I could bear, and I threw up. Mush appeared at my side, his arm on my back.

"We must help," he told me. "Even those who are dying."

I retched and retched, until the heaving subsided, and then I tried to control my breathing.

"COME ON!" I heard Sergeant Buckingham yell. "MOVE YOURSELVES!"

We spent an age trying to help the survivors, and longer still removing the dead. A company of white soldiers joined us, and I was left with a Private Sid Smith.

"We're in some trouble, here," he told me.

His hair was curly and ginger, and his pale skin freckled.

"Why must we run?" I asked. "Why don't we turn and fight?"

Private Smith shook his head.

"The Germans outnumber us," he replied. "I've heard perhaps two to one. And they've got more vehicles and weapons. I don't know who planned this expedition, but they want shooting."

I nodded and continued with my awful task. By nightfall, we were exhausted and demoralised, and I went to find Mush. He was camping with some others, close to the road. Behind, the mules were calm now, and their eyes shone in the darkness like ebony glass beads. The only light came from lit cigarettes and the occasional torch, and a stiff breeze that made the leaves rustle.

"These Germans are cowards," I said, my shock turning to rage. "Darn them and their planes. They should face us like men!"

"They are only doing their duty," Mush replied. "The same as us, brother."

I disagreed.

"No," I told him. "They are cowards who drop bombs on civilians. We do not do such things, Mush. We have honour!"

"We follow orders," he replied. "Just like them. It is the leaders who make the commands. We are merely the spokes on a wheel, brother. It is they who turn it."

I could not sleep. My mind was filled with blood and screams, and the incessant wailing of Stukas. I rose before dawn and washed my face in a nearby stream. As the cool water refreshed me, I sensed someone nearby. I turned to find Sid Smith, smiling.

"You're one of the muleteers," he said. I nodded and told him my name.

"A long way from home, then?"

"Yes," I replied.

"India?"

"The north," I told him. "A village, close to Rawalpindi."

"I'm from London," he said. "Tooting. Home's a

bit closer for me."

I splashed more water onto my face and then
through my hair. My feet were sore, and my legs
seemingly filled with lead, and my head thumped.

"I've never been to London," I told Sid. "I have
always wanted to go."

Sid grinned and the pale skin around his eyes
creased.

"Ain't many like you round my way," he replied.
"Although, I'm not one to hate a man because of his
skin. My old man fought at Cable Street."

"I don't understand."

"Oswald Mosely," said Sid. "He's a fascist and Nazi-
sympathiser. He wanted to march through the East End
of London, and the people stopped him at Cable Street.
It was a right good punch-up, according to my old man."

I was shocked. Was Sid saying that a fascist party
existed in England?

"But I thought we were fighting *against* fascists?" I
said. "How can there be some in England?"

"Who knows?" Sid replied. "Misguided, wrong-
headed? Don't matter to me. I hate 'em, and I'm happy
to fight 'em all, Khan."

"Me too," I said. "In India we have people who
want to side with the Germans. They want to remove
the British."

"Stands to reason you'd want us gone," said Sid. "We took your country from you."

My shock increased. Who was this white man, with his insubordinate views? I had never dreamt that such men could exist in Britain.

"I see your confusion," said Sid. "I'm a communist, Khan. But this war is about more than politics. It's about stopping the Germans before they conquer Europe."

"And communism?" I asked. "I have read much about Russia and Stalin."

"That's not my version of communism," Sid told me. "I just want a fairer country to go back to. We're cannon fodder, you and I. Told what to do by rich men who have never seen a battle themselves. It was the same last time, too."

"The Great War," I said, nodding.

"Stupid name for a war," said Sid. "Nothing great about it. It was slaughter, Khan."

"My grandfather fought here," I revealed. "Le Bassée, Neuve Chapelle and then the Somme."

"And he survived?"

I nodded.

"He was lucky," I replied. "Most of his friends died here. Many have never even been found. It was why I enlisted. After my grandfather passed away. . ."

"To serve the King?" Sid smirked. "I fight for my people, mate, not some toff in a crown."

"To help," I told him. "The Raj is all I have ever known. It is my duty to serve it."

Sid knelt beside me and began to wash his face.

"Better get moving," he eventually said. "The Jerries will be back at first light, and no mistake."

"Jerries?" I asked. Sergeant Buckingham had used the phrase too.

"Nickname for the Germans," Sid replied. "Although I can think of some other choice words for them!"

We walked back to camp together, to find everyone readying to march on.

"I'll see you down the road, then," said Sid.

"It would be a pleasure," I replied.

"Stay safe, Private Khan."

4

We continued northwards, via Béthune, and arrived at a town called Cassel two days later. We made for the grounds of a once-grand chateau, now fallen into disrepair, and set up camp. We were great in numbers, and the chateau grounds were not large enough to take us all, so some camped in a field instead. And, once again, we settled and tried to find some kind of normality.

I was hungry and tired but made sure to look after my three mules before taking care of myself. The animals were calm, but seemed sad to me, ridiculous as that may sound. I had learned much about them on our journey, however. Where they might nuzzle and playfully butt each other before, now they were still, their heads drooping. I found a grooming kit and began to remove their blankets and noticed that their coats were dulled and ragged.

"Don't worry, my friends," I whispered. "Fazal will see to you."

One by one, I groomed and cleaned them as best I could. Then I found a hoof pick and checked each of them. The journey had been hard, and I was wary of being kicked by them, so I took my time and found plenty of debris to remove. In India, we had carried field forges with us. These allowed us to re-shoe our mules on the go. But in France, we had not been issued forges, and so their hooves had taken great strain. All three needed shoes, but when I spoke to Sergeant Buckingham, he began to laugh.

"Impossible!" he told me. "Even if we had the shoes, we have no forges, Khan."

"But without the shoes, the mules will suffer," I told him.

"We're all suffering, Khan!" he bellowed. "I haven't the courage to look at my own feet, lest they be riddled with rot. Forget the beasts, man! We've got humans to consider."

When my face fell, he grew annoyed.

"Don't tell me you worship the useless things?" he said. "I had enough of cow-worshipping Hindustanis in Delhi!"

"I am a Muslim, sir," I replied. "We do not worship animals."

"Glad to hear it!" said Sergeant Buckingham.

I walked away in anger and despair. My mules were not desperate for new shoes, but if they didn't get them soon, they would find walking painful. And, like cars without wheels, mules with injured hooves were no good to any of us.

"What is the matter?" asked an older comrade called Sadiq.

He was from Rawalpindi like me, tall and strong, and wearing a regulation *pagri* – a turban – which consisted of cloth wrapped around a quilted cotton cone. When I relayed the Sergeant's words, Sadiq merely shook his head.

"What can you expect of people who steal other's countries?" he asked. "They do not care about us, never mind the animals."

"But the mules are just like us!" I insisted. "We have a duty to them."

"Nonsense!" Sadiq replied, smoothing his oiled moustache. "We have only one duty, Fazal. To stay alive in this hell."

"But. . ."

Sadiq shook his head again.

"Listen, brother," he said. "We are not alone in feeling this way. Do you believe that the white soldiers feel any differently? We came for victory, and we are running from the fight. Don't tell me about duty or honour. There is none to be had."

That night, I rested well. It had been many days since my last real sleep, and when morning came, I was groggy and grumpy. Mush awakened me, and together we walked to the latrines to relieve ourselves. Captain Ashdown was standing nearby, engaged in conversation with Sergeants Buckingham and Davis, and another Captain called Morrow. All four of them wore serious expressions, and their exchange seemed heated.

"I wonder what they are saying?" Mush whispered.

"I can't hear," I replied.

"More bad news, no doubt."

In the mess tent, we were given tea and biscuits, and some bread and jam. I scoffed mine quickly, and took an extra cup of tea, too.

"I am desperate to bathe," said Mush. "I feel dirty."

"Me too," I told him.

"I have not washed for days and my uniform is making me itch."

"Perhaps we will have time later," I suggested.

"If the Germans spot us here," Mush replied, "there will be no later."

With breakfast done, we headed for our tasks, rested and refreshed, and the sun broke through the clouds to further brighten the day. My mules were tethered close to our tent, and once again I began my grooming routine. They seemed happier and more relaxed after a quiet night, and again I could not help but compare our lots.

"Only, you did not choose this life, Baba," I told the pale brown one. "You did not choose anything."

One of the others reared its head and nudged me, and I returned the gesture. To my left, Mush began to laugh.

"They are mules, brother," he said, "not future wives!"

During late afternoon, I took a stroll around the grounds and found that the chateau was deserted. The main house was derelict, with fire damage to the rear, and fallen stonework. Rats scurried from an outhouse when I tried the door, giving me a fright. Further along, through a courtyard, I found Sergeant Buckingham smoking his pipe and reading a letter. He had removed his jacket and tie and unbuttoned his shirt and had his feet up on one chair as he sat on another. A hip flask of whiskey sat on a small table beside him, and his eyes were glazed.

"What are you doing, Khan?" he asked.

"Nothing, sir," I replied. "I was just taking a walk."

"Well, go elsewhere, will you?" he said. "I wanted some peace."

"Yes, sir," I replied, before making a hasty exit.

I wandered towards a small copse which led down to the river that ran behind the grounds. The water was clear and fresh, and I sat on the bank and daydreamed. Tranquillity seemed out of place, given our predicament, but it was very welcome. I must have been there a while before I spotted the boy. He stood on the opposite bank, holding a stick to which he'd tied some string. A fishing expedition. He must have been ten or eleven years old, with dark hair and eyes and a sallow complexion, as though he hadn't eaten enough.

"*Excusez-moi,*" the child said when he saw me, "*je ne voulais pas vous déranger.*"

The boy looked scared and unsure of himself. I shrugged and gestured to my mouth.

"I do not speak French," I told him.

The boy looked past me, and his eyes lit up. I turned to find Captain Ashdown standing behind me.

"He said he didn't mean to disturb you," the Captain explained, before turning to the boy. "*Vous ne devriez pas être ici.*"

The startled boy turned and fled, and I asked the Captain what he had said.

"I told him he shouldn't be here," he replied. "We can't have civilian children running about. There are live weapons around."

"You speak French?"

"Yes," he said. "Taught at school."

"In England?"

Captain Ashdown shook his head.

"No, Khan," he replied. "In India. I was born and raised there."

"I did not know that, sir," I replied. "Please forgive my mistake."

"At ease, Khan," the captain said. "There is no mistake to forgive."

I wondered whether to ask about our situation but decided against it. I was a private, and my orders would come when they were ready. Instead, I asked a more general question.

"How long will we rest here?"

"Not long," said Captain Ashdown. "I'm awaiting further details from England."

"The Germans are gaining ground?" I added.

"Yes," the Captain replied. "The enemy is closing in, Khan, and I think we might be in for a frightful battle."

"We are here to win," I said, remembering what Mush had said.

Captain Ashdown sat and smiled.

"Yes," he said, "but let's enjoy the peace for a while, shall we?"

I smiled in return and spoke again.

"Permission to bathe in the river, sir?"

The Captain nodded.

"You don't need my permission for everything," he told me.

I walked back to fetch Mush and wondered when our next brush with death would occur. We did not have to wait for very long.

5

The next morning, a local farmer arrived with a number of butchered chickens. He spoke with Captain Ashdown for a while, before the two of them shook hands. I was standing with Baba and my other mules, carrying out my chores with Sadiq, and the Captain beckoned to me.

"Monsieur Legrand has given us these chickens, Khan," he said. "I thought you and your fellows could cook something for yourselves. Something a touch Indian, perhaps?"

I glanced at the chickens and my stomach growled. Unlike most of the Punjabi men I knew, cooking was one of my special skills. In India, I had often helped the cooks in our company. However, the chickens had not been slaughtered in accordance with our religion. They were not *halal*. Then again, nor was the bully beef we had been eating, and not a single man had complained.

Perhaps, in such a perilous situation, we could be forgiven. Our need for a hearty meal was great.

I nodded.

"I would need onions and garlic and something to spice the dish with," I replied. "And we would need to prepare the chickens, of course."

Monsieur Legrand eyed me with interest, watching as I spoke to the Captain.

"You 'ave some English?" he said in a thick accent.

"Some," I said in my own strong accent.

"This is rare, no?" he added. "I met some Indian in 1915. They don't speak well English."

"Better than my French, sir," I replied, and the two of us returned smiles.

"We would need onions and garlic," Captain Ashdown told him.

"*Ce n'est pas un probléme!*" Legrand replied.

I may not have spoken French, but his meaning was clear.

"Do you have chillies?" I asked him. "Or spices?"

"Pardon?"

I looked to Captain Ashdown, but he simply shrugged.

"Chillies," I said more slowly.

I thought hard and then decided to mimic someone who'd eaten something a little too spicy.

"Like this," I said, waving a hand before my mouth and pretending to blow air.

When neither man reacted, I tried again, jumping up and down this time. Legrand and Captain Ashdown looked to each other and burst into laughter.

"*Il entend les piments et épices,*" the Captain finally said.

"*Oui oui!*" Legrand replied, clapping a meaty and calloused hand against my back. "You 'ave been fooled, yes?"

I shook my head and smiled. Captain Ashdown grinned.

"Sorry about that, old chap," he said. "I couldn't resist having a jape. Lovely impression of a *Memsahib* on her first day in Delhi, however!"

Legrand returned later with fat red chillies, onions and garlic, and green and black peppercorns. He had a young woman with him, his daughter perhaps, and some of the men suddenly discovered a greater interest in our conversation. The young woman wore a long grey dress and her head was covered with a blue scarf. She smiled at me, but said nothing else, as Legrand handed me his wares.

"This is all we have," he told me. "*Bon appétit!*"

"Thank you, sir," I replied, "and miss, too."

The two of them smiled once more, before going on their way.

"Careful," teased Sadiq, "you'll end up with French-speaking children!"

"Do not disrespect her that way," I replied, "she could be our sister."

Sadiq groaned.

"Calm down," he replied. "It was only a joke."

Sadiq was also a cook, both of us having learned from our mothers. He joined me, as we cleaned and portioned several chickens. I first removed the heads and feet, before cutting out the back bone and flattening each bird. Sadiq then cut each bird into eight parts – two breasts, two drumsticks, two thighs and two wings. Finally, we deskinned and deboned as many of the pieces as we could and threw the bones into pots. I began to chop up the garlic and onions, and some potatoes that had been left in the mess tent. Sadiq took oil and began to heat it, before crushing the peppercorns and chillies with a mortar and pestle, making a fiery paste.

"Some *masala* would be good," he said, "but this will do."

"It was decent of Monsieur Legrand to give us the chickens," I replied. "We can make do."

"As always, brother," said Sadiq.

We fried the bones and then added water, a touch of the paste and some onion, in order to make a stock.

This took about an hour, and in the meantime, we sat and joked and talked about our situation. Sergeant Buckingham entered the tent just as the stock was ready, and he sniffed the air.

"Oh dear," he said, seemingly drunk again. "Smells like India. . ."

I shrugged and pointed at the chickens.

"Captain Ashdown asked that we cook something traditional," I told him.

"Not *my* tradition," the Sergeant snapped. "What's wrong with a good old-fashioned chicken stew, Khan? I hadn't counted on being this close to Blighty and continuing to eat that muck you people call food."

I had no reply, so I waited for him to grow bored and leave. During that pause, I helped Sadiq to find three large pots and set the stock aside. Neither of us spoke. When Sergeant Buckingham finally left, I turned to Sadiq.

"He is always drunk," I said, and Sadiq nodded.

"Who can blame him," my friend replied, just as Mush walked in.

"Blame who, and for what?" Mush asked.

When I explained, Mush just laughed.

"How I would love to drink and forget this hell," he said.

"But it would be *haram*," I said, meaning impure.

Muslims were forbidden from alcohol, although I knew many who ignored the rules.

Mush scoffed.

"And is this chicken *halal*?" he asked. "We are in Europe, Fazal. We cannot live by every rule. It is not possible."

"I have not prayed once since Marseille," Sadiq told us. "Does that make me less of a Muslim?"

"No," I replied. "However, that cannot be helped. Drinking whiskey is something else."

We continued to discuss things as we fried the rest of the onions, garlic and paste, with me guiding Mush. Eventually we threw in the pieces of chicken and potatoes, browned them slightly, and then added the stock.

"Smells good," said Mush.

"Smells like home," I replied.

"No," Sadiq told me. "Nothing here smells of home."

The Stuka bombers returned before we could try our chicken, with little warning. One minute we were joking around, the next we were rushing for cover, as two bombs exploded all about us. I did not consider my actions, nor hesitate. I bolted from the mess, and raced towards my mules, desperate to get them to safety.

They were braying silently, and kicking out their legs, and it took some time to calm them. Another bomb exploded against the chateau and sent stone flying in all directions. Thankfully, we were out of range.

I untied the ropes, as Mush joined me, his face red and drenched in sweat.

"Hurry, brother!" he shouted. "There is another bomber overhead."

Dragging my mules away from the house was hard work, and time and again, I slipped and fell over. But, Baba soon realised I was helping them and began to put in the effort required. The other two followed his lead, just as I had always done with my real grandfather. It was as though he was with me, guiding me to safety. In that moment, and despite the danger, I realised how much I missed his gruff voice.

At the boundary of the chateau grounds, I relaxed just a little. Even though we were in the open, the bombers seemed to be targeting the central area, around the chateau itself. My comrades were racing to join me, and then a fourth huge explosion rocked the chateau, completely destroying the frontage.

Then, just as quickly as they had arrived, the bombers vanished. I looked about for casualties, but miraculously there were none. Just dazed and confused men standing in shock, and Captain Ashdown leading a team of soldiers, making sure everyone was safe. I turned to my mules and saw them noiselessly braying, and for once, I was glad of their silence. I knelt facing eastwards, closed my eyes, thought of my family and said a quick prayer.

6

We lost fifteen animals, mostly mules and a few horses, several tents, and much equipment, but not a single man. In itself, that was amazing, but when I saw how close we'd come, I was flabbergasted. One of the four bombs had hit the ground about thirty yards from the nearest men. And not a single one was seriously hurt. There were some minor cuts and grazes, but that was all.

"We have been blessed this day," Sadiq exclaimed. "*Inshallah*, we will escape this with our lives."

Many of my comrades were checking their animals, and the rest cleared debris and rubble. The officers were huddled together as dusk fell, and I decided to walk by and listen to their conversation. I worried that they might shout as I approached, but they were too busy discussing something called Operation Dynamo.

"Stands to reason," Sergeant Buckingham said. "That's why they sent us north."

"No," Captain Ashdown replied. "Our original mission was to supply the defensive lines, to try and stop the German advance through Belgium."

"I agree," said Captain Morrow. "This is purely about circumstances. London has made this call on the hoof, and no mistake."

"Well," said Buckingham, "let's not complain. I'm all for it."

"But there's nearly a quarter of a million men in France," said Captain Ashdown. "How in the name of God can we evacuate them *all*? The Jerries are right on our tail and won't just sit by and watch our escape."

As they went on, I pretended to look for something through a pile of rubble, and then watched as they finished their meeting. Captain Ashdown spotted me and came across.

"Private Khan," he said in a sombre tone. "I hope you weren't eavesdropping."

"No, sir," I lied. "I was merely. . ."

"Oh, never mind," said Ashdown. "You'll find out soon enough. Was the mess tent hit?"

"No, sir," I told him. "It is intact."

"Good," said the Captain. "Can you organise food for every man, within the next hour or so?"

"Yes, sir."

"And is there enough for tomorrow too?"

"There is more than enough," I explained.

"Excellent," he replied. "I'm awaiting orders, but it looks as though we're moving out. I want everyone on standby to leave within an hour of the order. Is that clear?"

"Yes, sir."

"And Private?"

"Sir. . .?"

"I like you," said Captain Ashdown. "You're a decent chap and hardworking. But don't ever lie to me again. It's insubordinate and will serve you no good."

"Yes, sir!"

I felt sheepish as he left, but I deserved it. Captain Ashdown was loyal and fair, and I had no right to lie to him.

Mush, Sadiq and I gathered our company, alongside Sergeants Buckingham and Davis's. The men were served quickly, and ate quickly, as darkness drew in. No one commented on the chicken, not even Buckingham, because there was no mood for it. And no time, either. After supper, we worked by torch and candlelight, gathering our belongings and remaining equipment, and getting ready to decamp.

Most of the tents came down, leaving only a few

into which most of the men were crammed. Not that we slept. We were too fearful of another bombing, and too apprehensive of the order to leave. None of us were map readers, but we knew that we'd almost reached the north-eastern coast of France. How could we push further, without reaching the sea? And once there, our backs to the Channel, we'd be sitting ducks for the Germans.

I recalled the word *evacuate* from the officers meeting I'd spied on and wondered what that meant. Where would we go? The only logical step would be east, into Northern Belgium, and into battle. Or west perhaps, and away from the German lines. The alternative was retreat to England, but that made no sense at all. It was a ridiculous notion. I grew fearful then, realising that we might be making a last stand at the coast, faced with a greater enemy, whose firepower and numbers outstripped our own. Two to one, Sid Smith had told me. I couldn't help but think that our end was in sight.

And that thought sent shivers of dread coursing through my body.

In the morning, I heard a commotion, close to the chateau entrance. There was shouting at first, and then a whistle, followed by the sound of vehicles and at least one motorbike. Fearing the worst, and without a weapon, I armed myself with a hoof pick. It was short but had a sharp spike, and if any German came close enough, it would make a good weapon.

Only, I need not have worried. As I edged closer, I saw Captain Ashdown shaking hands with another British officer, one I had never seen before. The two men exchanged pleasantries, and then the gates opened, and five vehicles entered the compound. They parked side by side and about twenty or so weary-looking troops jumped out. They were wide-eyed and dirty, and immediately asked for water and bread. Captain Morrow called to me.

"Private Khan," he said. "Any of that chicken left?"

"Yes, sir," I replied.

"Then gather some others and make sure these soldiers are fed," he ordered. "They've been fighting Jerry down the road."

I nodded and assembled some of my comrades at the mess. We poured the food into bowls, sliced bread, and served it all with butter and water. The soldiers were 8th Battalion Worcestershire Regiment, and most of them seemed friendly as they plodded into the mess. I took charge, making sure each was given a fair share of food, before dishing up for the officers.

"Really good of you, Private," said their captain,

whose name was Haywood. "And rather spicy, too. Very agreeable."

I left them to it, standing by the entrance. To my left, several of my fellow muleteers were talking in Punjabi, our native tongue. Eventually, a white soldier took exception.

"Here, here!" he called. "Let's not be having that! Speak English!"

A couple of his friends agreed, but my comrades ignored his request.

"I said speak English!" he insisted. "You foreigners!"

He had dark hair, shaved close to his scalp, and his uniform was thick with dried mud. I glanced at Captain Ashdown, who consulted with Haywood, before coming over.

"Is there something wrong?" he asked the argumentative soldier.

"No, sir," the soldier replied. "I just want to know what they're talking about."

"And why is that your concern?" asked Captain Ashdown.

"Because we're not in India, sir," the man replied, smirking at his friends.

Captain Ashdown sighed.

"Nor is this England," he pointed out, "and yet, here we are, and not a French sentence to be had."

"I don't speak French," the man replied. "We didn't

all get schooled, sir."

By now, the entire mess had tuned in, including my fellow muleteers.

"I am not responsible for your misfortune," Captain Ashdown told him. "But, I *am* responsible for my men. They have travelled thousands of miles to help our cause, and I will not see them disrespected. Is that clear, Private?"

The man bowed his head, his pale skin turning scarlet about the cheeks.

"*Private?*"

"Yes, sir," he sheepishly replied.

"Excellent," said Captain Ashdown. "Now finish your supper and get some rest. We've some hard days ahead of us and must stick together. No matter where we were born or schooled."

"Yes, sir."

"Oh, and Private," he added. "Should you smirk at me again, I shall recommend you for dishonourable discharge. Is that clear?"

"Yes, sir!"

7

Later that day, a member of 8th Battalion sought me out. I had walked down to the stream once more and was watching the sun glistening off the water. We had been ordered to head for Dunkirk, and I was killing time, my duties done. When I first saw the soldier, I thought he meant me harm, but I was wrong.

"I wanted to apologise for Watkins," he said, holding out his hand.

I shook it and shrugged, as the man sat next to me and pulled out a tobacco pipe. He tapped it against a rock several times, before inspecting it.

"There is nothing to apologise for," I replied. "He was tired, I'm sure."

"He's a pain in the backside," said the man, filling his pipe. "You're not the first person he's insulted. We met some Senegalese chaps, fighting for Frenchi and he took exception to them too. I'm Lieutenant Cummings, by the way."

"Private Khan," I replied. "Company 32 of Force K-6, Royal Indian Army Service Corps. Glad to meet you, sir."

"Rehearsing for when we're all taken prisoner?" joked Cummings.

"Is our situation so awful?" I asked.

"Absolutely," Cummings replied. "We've been fighting a rear-guard action for days. If we move any further north, we'll become fish. We've sustained major losses – men and armaments, and the Germans have got the beating of us. The situation could not be more serious, Khan."

"I was thinking the same thing, sir," I admitted, as I watched a brown mouse scurry across the opposite bank and disappear into a hole at the foot of an ancient tree. "And I'm fearful of what lies ahead."

"You're being sent to Dunkirk?"

"Yes," I told him. "After which, there is no land."

"Can you swim, Private Khan?"

"A little," I admitted. "Not enough to call it swimming."

"Then, here's hoping we don't have to swim for it!" he jested.

He was tall and broad shouldered in his uniform,

with sand-coloured, oiled hair and a wide, bulbous nose. His eyes were the palest blue I'd ever seen, and his forehead and cheeks freckled. His moustache was neat and clipped, and oiled too, and he had a deep pink scar across his left jawline. After a while, he spoke again.

"Always wondered what India was like."

I smiled at him.

"It is a beautiful place, sir," I told him. "My region is rich with fertile soil and plentiful rivers. And the weather is far better. The food, too, although you may disagree."

"Where are you from?"

"Rawalpindi, in the north."

"Ah," he said. "I'm from the English Midlands. A place called Malvern Wells. I miss it."

"I miss my home, too," I replied.

"Wife, children?" asked Cummings.

"No," I told him. "I am too young. You?"

Cummings seemed a little forlorn.

"My wife is called Ida, and we have Harry and James," he replied. "And little Beatrice – she's three years old. I fear that I may never see them again."

"I'm sorry to hear that," I told him.

"Do you ever worry that we might not make it?"

"Yes," I replied. "But that decision rests with someone else. I will simply carry out my duty. If I am to meet my end, so be it."

"Don't Hindustani's believe in reincarnation?" said Cummings.

"I am a Muslim, sir," I explained. "We do not believe in that. We believe in Paradise, much like a Christian Heaven."

Cummings glanced at me.

"Thanks for clearing up my ignorance," he said, his expression genuine. "I'm fascinated by other religions and cultures. Met a Buddhist in London last year. A very fine fellow. I'm not sure I believe in anything, however. War certainly shakes a man's faith."

"It does," I replied. "But we must try, sir."

"Perhaps I will visit India one day," he said. "When all of this madness ends, of course. Seems a distant dream, just now."

We sat a little longer, before I heard Mush calling for me.

"I must go, sir," I said. "Thank you for sitting with me."

"No, no," said Cummings. "The pleasure was all mine. *Bonne chance*, as the French would say."

"Does that mean good luck?" I asked.

"Indeed," Cummings replied.

"Then *bonne chance* to you, too, sir."

*

Captain Ashdown gathered us together and broke the news we had expected. We were ready to move, and he wanted us to be aware of what might await us. His translator stood by him, as always.

"The Germans have outflanked us," he admitted. "They are now east and south of us, and drawing in. I've spoken to Command, and it seems we're in a pickle."

Beside me, Mush began to chuckle.

"So very English," he whispered. "Why does pickle signify danger to these people? My wife's pickle is dangerous but only because she puts so much chilli into it!"

"Idiot!" I whispered in return.

"Operation Dynamo has been given the go-ahead," Captain Ashdown continued. "We will make our way to Dunkirk, and there, we will be evacuated to England..."

The men began to murmur. Some wore fearful expressions – wide-eyed and slack-jawed.

"As long as we stick together and follow orders, we will stand a good chance," the Captain added. "But I must warn you that the road will be difficult, and we will face great danger."

He cleared his throat.

"This is not what we expected, men, and certainly

not ideal," he said. "But, our orders are clear, and we must obey them. We move out in five minutes."

Again, the men murmured fearfully, and I took Mush aside.

"This is nothing but a retreat," he told me. "There is no honour in this!"

"It is practical," I countered. "We must survive."

"We should turn and fight," said Mush. "We cannot run away like beaten dogs."

I sighed.

"What else can we do?" I asked. "We *are* beaten."

Part of me felt as Mush did, but I was also excited at the prospect of visiting England and seeing its glory for myself. My grandfather had been hospitalised in Brighton during the Great War, and I longed to see it and London too. I wondered if I might get the chance. Mush seemed agitated, however, and remained angry.

"So much for this great British army," he whispered. "How did they ever seize our country?"

I kept quiet and left him there, fuming. I found my mules and checked them one last time.

"Here we go again," I said to Baba, as I heard the call to ship out. "Don't worry, friend. I will not leave you behind."

Baba nudged me with his head, and I patted his

haunches in return. A hundred yards away, Cummings held up his hand in farewell. I returned the gesture before setting off.

8

Cassel was barely twenty miles from Dunkirk, and we should have made it sooner. Only, the roads were now packed with local civilians, and fellow troops from the British Expeditionary Force – thousands and thousands of them. Abandoned and ruined vehicles lined the route, yet more evidence of our retreat. As we slowly progressed, I saw evidence of bombs and many casualties. Here and there, medics tried to help soldiers and civilians, but many were beyond saving.

Elsewhere, we saw ragged and scared locals, bewildered by the turn of events. I sensed an air of shock and dismay, and perhaps anger comparable to that we'd experienced on leaving Marseille. Many cast suspicious glances our way, and on one occasion, a boy threw stones at us. I could not fault their sense of betrayal, but I could not condone it either. We were losing the fight, and we had to try and save ourselves. Perhaps return to fight another day.

I thought back to my childhood, and my school days. I had changed schools, to one that better suited my parents' aspirations for my future. Two local boys, both older, took an instant dislike to me. I had been eight years old then, and the bullies terrified and tormented me. One evening, I cried in front of my grandfather, and he took me in his arms.

"What's the matter, child?" he asked.

He was a bear of a man, with a barrel-chest and huge arms and hands. But his eyes remained soft, at least in my presence, and he had never raised his voice to me. He preferred patience and explanation to physical punishment, unlike my parents. Looking back, I wondered if his distaste for violence stemmed from his experiences of war.

I told him of the bullies, and he shook his head.

"You are weak, Fazal," he told me. "Your arms are too skinny and your legs scrawny. We must build you up, if you are to defeat these boys."

Only, I did not want to defeat them. I only wished for them to leave me in peace. But my grandfather was not to be denied. He began to train me: running and gymnastics, and basic self-defence and boxing skills. In the meantime, he explained that there was no shame in walking away from a fight.

"You must weigh the odds," he told me. "If they are not in your favour, you run away and await your time. It will come—"

However, the first time I ran, I was ridiculed as a weakling by my schoolmates. I gained a reputation for being spineless, and this only encouraged the bullies. But, I remembered my grandfather's advice, putting up with the bullying and derision for two entire school years. In that time, I grew stronger and more determined, but I did not let it show.

Finally, I was ready to confront the boys – Mohammed and Nazir –and they had no inkling of my new-found strength. I felt older and more confident, too, and ready to take on anything.

One afternoon, they accosted me as school finished. We were made to wear shorts, as English schoolboys did, and caps too. Nazir grabbed my cap in a crowded yard and threw it into the air. Meanwhile, Mohammed tried to pull down my shorts. The other boys egged them on, and I grew angry.

"Please don't," I asked them. "I do not wish to fight you."

Nazir mimicked my words.

"Look at the girl!" Mohammed added. "Shall we dress you in women's clothes and make you dance?"

I shook my head.

"I do not wish to fight you," I said again.

Only, neither bully was willing to listen. Without warning, I punched Nazir on the nose, and he let out a cry and began to wail. The other boys grew instantly silent, staring at me in disbelief. Mohammed moved to strike me, but I stepped aside and placed him in an armlock, shoving him headfirst into a hedge. When I let go, he sprang to his feet and came again.

I swept his legs away and he landed on his backside, his humiliation complete.

"Please," I repeated a third time. "I do not wish to fight."

And with that, I picked up my cap and my school bag, and walked away. Neither boy bothered me again, and my reputation amongst my schoolmates improved dramatically. When I told my grandfather, he ruffled my hair, but also issued a warning.

"Don't become a bully yourself," he said. "Ego and pride are enemies of decency. You stood your ground, and that is wonderful. But only fight if you must. Fighting should always be the very last resort."

Now, I found myself remembering my grandfather's words once more. And I let go of any shame or humiliation I was feeling. Ego and pride would not help me to survive. Running away would.

*

The first air assault occurred moments later, and I was not ready for it, Daydreaming had left me exposed. The sudden droning of hornet-like Stukas snapped me to my senses.

"ENEMY PLANES!" yelled someone behind me.

The bullets came thick and fast, as the fighters swept low and raked the road with machine gun fire. Several civilians and soldiers fell, and I darted left, pulling my mules with me. They did not hesitate, and we bounded into the treeline. All around me others followed, screaming and wailing, and trying to escape with their lives. On the road, the Stukas made a second pass, higher this time, and dropped their payloads. Three separate explosions knocked me from my feet, and reduced visibility to almost nothing. The air was thick with smoke and dust and pierced by the cries of the wounded.

Shell-shocked and deafened, I crawled forwards, and tried to get my bearings. As the smoke began to clear a little, I saw a little girl, no more than five or six, lying motionless and bloody on the ground. Her mother lay close by, eyes wide open and life gone. I called out for a medic, but none appeared, so I tended to the child myself. She was unconscious but breathing and had only a flesh wound. I sat up, removed my jacket and covered her mother, lest the girl awaken and see her lying dead.

It took until nightfall for us to assess our losses, and again, we were lucky. Not a single member of the company nor any animal had been hurt, most of them making cover well before the Stukas closed in. Civilian casualties, on the other hand, were great because many of the locals had hidden under and behind carts and motorised vehicles. The carnage was sickening, and as more soldiers arrived on the scene, we began the sorry task of removing the dead and leaving the wounded by the roadside.

"We must move on," Captain Ashdown insisted. "Those are my orders. We cannot risk being caught."

When some of the men complained, the captain held his temper. He looked as sad as the rest of us, and just as guilty.

"I cannot accept this," said Mush as we found each other. "It is shameful to leave them."

"But we must," I told him, even though I agreed with every word.

"We will answer for this," he replied. "On the Day of Judgement."

I turned away, unable to offer any response.

And so, under cover of darkness, we left the injured civilians behind, and my spirits fell once more. Never had our motto of *Hukam Hai* felt hollower.

9

The second attack came next morning, as we closed in on Dunkirk. I was tending to my mules, having slept only fitfully and rising before dawn. Weariness infected the men, and each of us wore haunted expressions, as though we might already have died. I heard the droning long before the Stukas arrived, but that was all the warning I required.

"ENEMY!" I yelled, trying to rouse my sleeping comrades.

Captain Ashdown had not slept at all. He was some thirty yards away, drinking tea and reading a letter.

"Khan!" he screamed. "Get the animals and men into the woods!"

It felt like a recurring nightmare. Marching, hearing the bombers, finding shelter on the roadside amongst the trees and bushes, emerging to find destruction and death. An endless cycle of terror and despair. Once again, I led Baba and the others off the road, but this time, cover was sporadic and light, and we were easy targets. Hundreds of my comrades leapt to their feet and did the same, stumbling and falling and as panicked as stampeding water buffalo.

It was a terrible scene, with soldiers and civilians scattering once more, desperate to stay alive in the Germans' onslaught. From my position, I watched my fellow humans fall under machine-gun fire, and then three thumps, one after the other, and explosions and then ringing ears and temporary silence. I shook my head and ran to help, but Captain Ashdown ordered me to halt.

"Don't be a fool!" he hollered. "Wait!"

When it became clear that the bombers had moved on to new targets, the captain led the way, but there was little to be done. Another officer joined him, and they began to discuss something, as the rest of my company emerged. Captain Ashdown was angry and animated, but his fellow officer remained calm, merely shaking his head. He produced a slip of paper for Ashdown to read.

"Can you hear them?" Mush asked, appearing at my side. His face was streaked with dirt and his breath was as stale as my own.

"No," I replied. "Have we lost any men?"

Mush shrugged.

"It does not seem so," he told me.

In the distance, I heard more thuds, followed by explosions. I wondered how many troops were on the road to Dunkirk, and how many casualties we had sustained.

"They are closing in," said Mush. "From all directions."

"No," I replied. "Not from the north. That is where our troops are. The Germans are only bombing the road to Dunkirk. They have not reached the town. *Yet.*"

Captain Ashdown removed his cap and lowered his head. He appeared saddened and dismayed, and when he returned to us, he did not look us in the eye.

"We've been ordered to cut them loose," he said softly.

"Whom?" I asked.

He seemed to regain his composure in an instant, standing tall and replacing his peaked cap.

"The animals," he said, his tone gaining confidence.

"But. . ." said Mush.

"They are too burdensome," said Captain Ashdown. "And we cannot take them with us."

"But, that is not right," I said.

"I'm sorry, Khan," the Captain replied, too saddened to notice my insolence. "I cannot disobey direct orders."

I shook my head.

"How can we just leave them behind?" I asked. "Where will they go?"

Captain Ashdown lowered his head again.

"I'm sure the locals will have them," he replied. "We have no choice, Khan. Our orders are clear.

Sergeant Buckingham approached, and could not have been less sympathetic. He was drunk again, and grinning.

"About time, if you ask me," he said. "I don't know why we came this far with the darned things. Sheer luck that we haven't lost men whilst herding the useless things."

I almost snapped but thought better of it. There was no use in getting myself court-martialled for insulting a sergeant. Yet, that is exactly what I wished to do. How could Buckingham think the mules useless? They had been our faithful servants, enduring as much hardship as any of us. We had mutilated them, and taken away their voices, and for what? To turn them loose when they became a *burden*? It was cold-hearted and wicked, and I hated the very idea.

"We should have eaten them," Buckingham added, before winking at me. "Or is mule stew against your religion, Private Khan?"

Captain Ashdown cleared his throat.

"Perhaps you'd be best served organising the men, Sergeant?" he suggested.

"Yes, sir," said Buckingham, with barely disguised insolence.

Captain Ashdown ignored his reaction and took me aside once he'd gone.

"I don't like this any more than you," he admitted. "It sticks in my throat. These animals have served us since India, and I'm saddened to see them discarded in such a pitiless manner. But we must follow orders, Khan. No matter what our personal feelings."

"And if they discard us next, sir?" I asked.

For, were we not as voiceless and burdensome as our animals? And, in the eyes of men like Buckingham, just as lowly and dispensable?

"That will not happen," Captain Ashdown insisted. "I can assure you of that."

"Yes, sir," I replied. "Permission to speak freely, sir?"

Captain Ashdown nodded.

"This order angers me and makes me despair," I admitted.

"Duly noted, Khan," Captain Ashdown replied. "Thank you for your candour. Now, please carry on."

"Yes, sir!" I said.

*

I trudged back to Baba and the others and stood beside them for a long while. I rubbed their snouts and brushed their coats, and whispered sorry, over and over again. Baba stamped his front legs and pushed into my midriff with his head, and I grew even gloomier. Many people thought mules ugly and awkward, but to me they had proved their magnificence. They had been loyal and hardworking since our departure from India, despite their obstinate natures. Never failing us, never causing us problems, never ceasing to carry all that we laid upon their shoulders. They were as much our comrades as any man, and yet we were to betray them.

"This is awful," said Mush as he joined me. "Such a cruel waste."

"They will die," I replied. "I am certain of it. Who will care for them and feed them once we are gone?"

"Perhaps the civilians will have use for them?" Mush suggested.

"No, brother," I told him. "We are leaving the civilians behind too. They will be busy trying to escape the Germans. What use will they have for additional hungry mouths?"

"I can't bear to think of it," said Mush.

"Nor me," I told him. "It feels immoral."

"Remember when we first began to train with them?" asked Mush.

"Yes," I nodded. "They seemed so smelly and pointless. I wanted to be a soldier, not a muleteer. I had expected a gun and instead I got. . ."

"A dumb animal!" Mush said with a smile.

"Not so dumb," I replied. "Well, not until they were mutilated."

"I wonder if we will answer for this?" said Mush. "On the Day of Judgement. I wonder if their fate will determine ours?"

I shrugged.

"We are not doing this," I pointed out. "We did not give the order."

Mush stroked Baba and gave a wry smile.

"We are not so different to these beasts," he said. "We are but dumb animals, forced to follow orders and with no right of reply."

"At least we will get a chance to survive," I told him. "And we are not being abandoned to this war and all of its brutality."

Only, that was not entirely true. And I would learn as much once we finally reached Dunkirk itself.

I left Baba and the others untethered by a thick oak tree. They stood still for a moment, and then began to walk towards me.

"No, no," I told them. "This is where your journey ends, brothers. Stay."

But they were mules, not dogs, and they did not listen to my command. Instead, they formed a line, with Baba at its head, and did what they always did.

"Please!" I said, placing my forehead against Baba's warm and prickly snout. "We cannot take you, my friends. I am sorry."

A civilian family happened to trudge past. A father, a mother and two young sons, each of them weighed down with all that was left of their possessions. I gestured to the mules.

"Take them!" I said.

The father, short and strong, and with a red face, gave me a quizzical look.

"*Je ne comprends pas*," he said, and again, I understood without knowing the words.

"They are yours," I said, gesturing to the mules.

"What is?" asked the mother in heavily accented English. She stood three inches taller than her husband, her face worn by stress and fear. One of her boys held onto her dress and eyed me with fascination.

I took Baba's rope and led my friend to her.

"Please," I said, handing her the rope. "He is yours."

I pointed to Baba, and then to the women.

"Yours, madam. . ."

Suddenly she understood, and her features exploded with gratitude.

"*Oh, merci, monsieur!*" she said to me. "*Merci!*"

I shrugged and patted Baba on his snout.

"Goodbye friend," I whispered, and in my head I was addressing my grandfather too. "Perhaps we will meet again, down the road somewhere?"

As I left them there, Baba stood and brayed silently, and my heart broke. I wiped away tears and plodded back to the main road.

10

Dunkirk was decimated. I do not know what I expected, but what we found was a vision from Hell. Thousands of troops walked two abreast, towards the coast. A snaking line of ragged and malnourished soldiers and support staff, all of them anxiously awaiting an unknown fate, every face weathered and filthy.

In the distance, I heard guns. German troops were shelling the area all around us, which meant that they were closer than I had feared. Captain Ashdown had said our force was a quarter of a million strong. Were all of us caught here, I wondered. Outflanked and trapped by an enemy that seemed relentless and advanced with lightning speed? With our backs to the sea, were we simply awaiting the finality of death's touch?

"Jesus Christ!" Captain Morrow exclaimed. "This is insanity!"

Captain Ashdown merely shrugged.

"Let's just get on," he insisted.

The road we marched along was dotted with fallen comrades and civilians. To our left was a single-storey row of warehouses, bombed out and smouldering. To the right, and further along, a senior British officer urged everyone forward.

"Keep those spirits up, chaps!" he said. "Soon be over!"

His uniform was pristine – not a single mark upon it. I wondered if he had seen any action at all and doubted it. He looked like he'd stepped from an officer's club in Bombay.

"Come along now!"

As we approached him, he raised an eyebrow and called Captains Ashdown and Morrow across. Behind him, sat the ruins of a military truck. It had fallen to one side, its tarpaulin load cover burnt away, revealing only a charred frame. A couple of soldiers were dragging bodies clear, rags tied over their mouths and noses. More casualties lay around the vehicle, covered in jackets and blankets.

"Can you see them, brother?" Mush asked beside me. "So many dead."

Sadiq was with us, and he pointed towards a taller building on the left. It had also been bombed, the windows blown out. Thick grey smoke poured from the roofline.

"This was recent," said Sadiq. "Keep your wits about you. We have no weapons and no cover. We are an easy target for the Germans."

I turned to check on Captain Ashdown and found him remonstrating with the senior officer.

"What now?" I asked.

"Huh?" said Mush.

I pointed in the captain's direction.

"Who knows what they talk about?" Mush replied. "Just more white men deciding our future for us."

"Captain Ashdown is as Indian as any of us," I said. "He is not like some of the others."

Both Mush and Sadiq shook their heads.

"This is not our fight," said Sadiq. "This is about one white man fighting with another, and both have enslaved people just like us. Wake up, boy!"

But that was too simplistic, and I told them so.

"That may be true," I replied, "but we must still defend ourselves and our country. Do you think Hitler will stop at Europe? He has signed an agreement with the Japanese Emperor, and if we are not careful, they will overrun India too."

"But that means nothing here!" said Sadiq. "We are

not defending India. We are thousands of miles away, running like frightened dogs!"

I thought of my grandfather and his words.

"We will fight another day," I told them. "There is no shame in running to survive. What good are we to anyone if we die?"

I looked Mush in the eyes, hoping he'd remember what he said about surviving for the sake of his wife and children.

"Weasel words," said Sadiq. "This is what happens if you spend your time speaking in English with your masters."

"What do you mean?" I asked, suddenly angered.

"You have become confused, boy," Sadiq continued. "You think you are special to them, because of your language skills."

"No," I countered. "You are mistaken."

Sadiq sneered, and in that moment, he reminded me of Sergeant Buckingham – full of rage and hatred. Perhaps the war had already beaten both of them.

"You are no better than us!" Sadiq spat.

"But, I don't think of myself that way!" I insisted.

"Then why do you parrot Captain Ashdown?" he asked. "Repeating the same tired old lies about this shameful retreat?"

I shook my head.

"Because the Captain is right," I told him. "Because unless we run, we will die. It is called pragmatism, Sadiq."

"It is cowardice," Sadiq quickly replied. "And you, you are a white man's tool and nothing more. . ."

I turned away, stung by his accusations and angered too. This was no time to argue amongst ourselves. We needed to stick together. Anything less would see us facing dire consequences.

"I wish the two of you would shut your mouths!" Mush told us. "Whining like children. Who cares about right and wrong now? Let us deal with what Allah has put before us."

Sadiq lit a cigarette and turned away from us.

"Imbecile!" said Mush. "And *you*, why did you antagonise the fool?"

I shrugged.

"Because I am not what he says," I replied. "And because I learned long ago that bullies must never be allowed to prosper."

"Oh, be quiet!" said Mush. "As if we haven't enough to contend with."

A while later, Captain Ashdown told us to rest. We stood in a once pretty square, one side of it completely flattened. A dry fountain stood at the centre, surrounded by stone steps. Some soldiers were resting there, one of them having interlocked three rifles, so that they stood facing upwards without falling. He lay on his back, using his pack for a pillow and reading an English newspaper. Beside him, several of his colleagues napped. A lone officer sat ten yards from them, dipping his razor into a tin cup and shaving his cheeks whilst looking at a compact mirror.

"Looks like we've arrived then," said Mush. "Let's see what happens now."

"What do you mean?" I asked.

Mush smoothed his moustache, as we sat on the steps of a once grand hotel, its frontage tattered and ruined, and contents long since looted.

"Look around," he told me. "Can you sense any urgency? Is there any sort of plan here?"

He was right. No one seemed to be in absolute command. No one was going around the troops, organising and issuing orders. We had found ourselves in a lull, in the dreaded doldrums that I had read of in my favourite pirate stories as child. There was no wind in our sails, and no course for us to navigate. We were becalmed, and it felt strange and unreal.

And, as my pirate stories had taught me, even when becalmed, storms were never very far away.

11

My mother's best friend was a Sikh. A woman whose family lived beside ours. On Sunday mornings, the two of them would bake paratha together – thick or doubled chapattis stuffed with spiced onions and potatoes, or various fresh herbs. Our families would gather at each house alternately, where my grandfather and his counterpart, Mr Singh, would share stories of the Great War and their time in Europe.

The table would be laden with piles of fresh butter, paratha, tangy yoghurt and pickles of all kinds, and spicy, sugary tea made from water buffalo milk. Most Sundays I would be awakened by the aroma, and my stomach would ache until I took my first bite. I'd join my neighbours' children, and we would feast until our bellies came close to bursting. Then we'd lie down and chatter or read stories until we had digested enough to play outdoors.

As I opened my eyes, I could almost smell and taste those Sunday mornings, now so far away that they felt like another lifetime. Mush dozed beside me, dribbling onto his round-necked, buttoned collar. We can't have slept long but it was enough for me to dream of home comforts. As I sat up, Mush began to stir and then opened his eyes.

"I've been dreaming of mangoes," he sleepily told me. "Big, fat, juicy mangoes dripping like presents from Paradise."

I grinned.

"Parathas for me," I told him. "Sunday mornings and parathas."

He sat too and gestured towards the white soldiers.

"I wonder what they miss?" he said.

"Who knows?" I replied. "But they are just like us. No more or less men than us."

I thought about Sadiq's cruel words earlier.

"Do you think I'm as Sadiq said?" I asked.

Mush shook his head.

"You are simply different," he replied. "And why not? We can't all be the same, with the same ideas about the world. I just want to go home. I don't care who or what we fight for, or why. I just want to see Rawalpindi again."

"Me too," I told him. "But I also want to visit England, and to see more of France too."

Mush grimaced at the idea.

"England, yes," he said. "But I have had enough of France for now. Perhaps, when this is over, I will return to see more. All France has given me is fear and anxiety, and nightmares."

Several pockets of fellow muleteers surrounded us, all of them either napping, or busy chatting and waiting for something to unfold. The British soldiers did the same, killing time, waiting for orders from somewhere.

"Have you seen Captain Ashdown?" asked Mush.

"How?" I asked. "I've been asleep, just like you."

"I wonder where he has gone?" said Mush. "Perhaps the officers have better places to be – warm and dry with tea and cake, perhaps?"

"We should try and find some food," I told him. "Maybe some of the shops have supplies."

We stood and dusted ourselves down, before setting off around the square. Every building lay deserted, with soldiers and civilians lying everywhere, or sitting and playing with dice and cards, or reading books and newspapers. Some of the British greeted us with warmth, and I returned their kindness, but many others scowled as Mush and I passed them by. Some drank from wine bottles and tankards, and the air seemed tense with restlessness. Tables and chairs had been overturned, and windows smashed with rocks, rather than blown out by explosions.

"Ey up!" shouted one skinny young man from outside a bakery. "It's Gunga Din and his servant, lads!"

I did not understand the insult, only that it was one, and Mush began to bristle in anger.

"Look at him," he said, clenching his massive fists. "Skin and bones, and those wretched teeth. I should slap him until he cries!"

"No," I said. "We are outnumbered. Besides, he is just one fool. Ignore him."

It soon became clear that the shops had been emptied of anything useful. There was no food, no water, nor any other basics like soap or toothpaste, or razors even.

"Have we got anything at all?" asked Mush.

I found a lump of hardtack biscuit and a stick of sugar candy in my pocket.

"I was saving these," I told him. "But you are free to have them."

As Mush took my offerings, we turned off the square, past some scared civilians, and into a narrow and cobbled lane. Further along, a young boy saw us approaching and smiled.

"Hello soldiers," he said in a thick French accent. "You have something for me?"

"No, boy," I told him. "We are looking for food and water."

The boy pulled a face, said something in French and ran off, eager to find more soldiers no doubt.

"Shall we go back?" asked Mush. "This is pointless."

"We're just sitting around," I told him. "Let's explore a little."

We continued walking around the lanes that led from the square, but always within sight of it. At some point an order would come, and I wanted to be ready. We passed many little doorways, and more empty shops and cafes, and then happened upon a bar where several British soldiers were sitting, drinking.

"Have a drink, lads!" said one of them. "The Frenchies won't be needing it. Just help yourselves – we have!"

I was about to explain that we were Muslims but stopped short. Something in the demeanour of these men, and the condition of the bar itself made me wary.

"Let's go," I said to Mush.

"Why?" he asked.

"Look at the building," I told him. "They've smashed the door in and looted it. And there is an unconscious civilian on the floor, just inside the entrance."

Mush nodded when he saw what I had seen.

"This is not right," I continued. "We should not be looting from our allies – certainly not civilians. We are supposed to be helping them."

Mush nodded again.

"Agreed," he said. "Let's go."

As we hurried away, I heard raucous laughter and then glass breaking and wood splintering.

"What are those idiots doing?" said Mush, as we re-entered the square.

"I don't know," I replied. "But I don't want any part of it."

Moments later, a group of officers and soldiers appeared and ran down the lane we had just left. I heard shouting and yelling, whistles blowing and more barked orders. I had witnessed several riots in Rawalpindi, and this felt the same.

"Right, men!" I heard Captain Morrow call. "Fall in at once!"

As we assembled, more officers and a French military police unit ran towards the trouble, truncheons drawn and whistles at the ready.

"This will end badly," said Mush. "You wait and see."

12

We reassembled in the square. In all, we were still four hundred strong, having miraculously lost no men on our travels. Companies 25 and 29 were also heading to Dunkirk, so I'd learned, and I wondered how they had fared since Marseille. Only one company from Force K-6 was not being evacuated. Company 22 had been redeployed to the Saar region instead, to help with the fight against the Germans, and I felt a pang of guilt when I thought of them engaged in battle whilst we fled.

Captain Ashdown appeared with Sergeant Buckingham and seemed shaken. His face was paler and his expression sombre, as though he had received bad news from Command. Buckingham was the exact opposite, cheery and nonchalant despite our predicament. I struggled to understand why they showed such opposing moods.

"We will have orders very soon," Captain Ashdown told us. "Until then, and in light of events nearby, we're relocating to an area called Malo-les-Bains, just east of the town itself. We move out in five minutes."

Someone called out to say that we were thirsty and hungry, and Sergeant Buckingham grew enraged.

"SILENCE!" he yelled. "INSUBORDINATION WILL NOT BE TOLERATED!"

I turned to Mush and whispered.

"He is always well lubricated," I joked, and Mush smiled.

"Brother," he said, "I bet he has alcohol coursing through his veins."

Captain Ashdown held up a hand.

"I appreciate your hardship," he told us. "I will arrange for some supplies soon. Until then salvage what you can, and drink and eat sparingly. It's going to be a tough ride from here."

Captain Morrow approached and whispered something in Ashdown's ear, and then the two men seemed to argue. Yet again, I knew we were being kept in the dark. Something had happened whilst we were resting in the square, and I wanted to know what it was. Only, who could I ask?

A short while later, we filed out of the square and down another ruined street full of smouldering vehicles and bomb-damaged buildings. Here and there, frightened civilians appeared from doorways, but we did not stop for them. Besides, what could we offer them? We were as much refugees as they.

"HALT!" called Sergeant Buckingham. "Supply vehicles coming through!"

We stepped aside, allowing the trucks to pass by; two of them, both carrying oil drums. They reached a crossroads ahead of us and came to a stop. From somewhere to my left, anti-aircraft guns began to pound, and whistles were blown across the town. Suddenly, I heard engines droning, drawing in as we stood in the open.

"COVER!" I yelled before any of the officers could react.

Then I shouted again, only this time in Punjabi. The company scattered, taking refuge in already-destroyed buildings, as a German Hcinkel bomber and two Stukas appeared to the north-east. The smaller Stukas were mobile and rapid and soon upon us, their machine guns strafing us with a seemingly unending round of bullets. I grabbed Mush and we made it inside a café, just as the ground we'd been standing on was torn apart. Several civilians attempted to dash across the street but were mown down by a truck. The driver slammed on his breaks but all too late, and he was killed by a direct hit.

And then the larger plane struck. One bomb, perfectly placed, right between the oil supply trucks. The explosion was massive, as hundreds of gallons of fuel ignited instantly, thick dust and black smoke plumes throwing everything into semi-darkness. I struggled to catch my breath and fumbled about, praying that Mush was safe.

"Brother!" I yelled. "Mush!"

A part of the ceiling had caved in and landed on Mush's left leg. As the smoke cleared a little, I saw him trying to struggle free and crawled over to help.

"Are you okay?" I asked, as I pushed a narrow wooden beam away.

"Fine!" he shouted. "Nothing broken."

I helped him to stand, and together we edged towards the street, wary of another strike.

"We're done for," said Mush. "There is no way we will survive this."

"Courage!" I replied. "We have to stay strong."

Overhead, the whining of Stukas drew close again, and from the gloom, a party of soldiers appeared, carrying rifles. Two of them rushed towards us and took cover inside the café.

"Are you armed?" asked one of them.

"No," I told him. "We're service corps – no weapons."

"Then get out of the way!" the man yelled. "We're

under heavy fire."

He rolled out onto the street, and his mate followed close behind. As the planes passed overhead, they fired their rifles, trying in vain to score a direct hit.

"What are they doing?" asked Mush. "They cannot hope to. . ."

A thud and another explosion sent us tumbling once more, as the centre of the street erupted in a mess of concrete and sand and rocks. Our refuge saved us, but the two riflemen were not so lucky. All that remained of them were tin hats and a single boot.

"What now?" asked Mush.

"We wait," I told him.

We sat still for close to thirty minutes, as several bombs dropped close by. Each detonation caused shockwaves that made the building shudder and groan. More than once, I thought it would crash down upon us, but it did not. Outside, I could hear screaming and shouting, and then a platoon of soldiers arrived, and took positions up and down the street. Yet, not a single one carried anything larger than a rifle. It all seemed so ridiculous, so pointless.

"If this is the plan," said Mush, "then we might as well turn and fight. I will not die this way."

"Fight with what?" I asked him. "We have no weapons, brother."

Mush sat with his back to a wall, his face cut just above the left eye and trickling blood. I pulled a discarded table cloth towards us and tore off a strip. The cloth was checked blue and white, and when I wrapped it around his head, Mush grinned.

"It is only a flesh wound," he told me. "No need for a fuss."

"Be quiet," I replied. "How will you see with blood seeping into your eye?"

Outside, all was quiet now, and I decided to take a chance.

"Wait here," I told him. "Let me go and make sure we are clear."

"No," he told me. "We stay together, or we leave together. No argument!"

I nodded, and we stood again and crept out of the café. Two soldiers came out of the hotel next door when they saw us.

"Any more planes?" one of them asked. His stripes told me that he was a captain, so I gave him a salute.

"I cannot hear any, sir," I replied, failing to add that I could not hear anything much.

My ears still rang from the assault, and my eyes were gritty.

"I think some of your lot headed east," the captain told me. "You're probably best getting off this street.

And the enemy will be back before you know it."

"Which way to Malo-les-Bains, sir?" I asked.

"Go right at the junction," he replied. "But mind the burning trucks and watch out for German shells. They're closing in fast."

"Thank you, sir!"

"No need for thanks, Private," the man replied. "I just wish they had given you guns. Not much use without them."

I thanked him again, said a prayer for luck, and then Mush and I headed out, eager to be reunited with our own company.

13

We followed the streets and lanes eastwards, as we had been directed, and found more devastation. Not a single street had escaped the bombs. Most of them were littered with abandoned vehicles and weapons, and even a few anti-aircraft guns. Several trams lay empty, the tracks blown apart and passengers long gone. One had been blown onto its side, and still smoked.

Sadly, we saw bodies at every turn. Young and old, civilian and military. It pains me to think of those dead souls, so I cannot describe them. It would be heartless. The cost of our retreat became clearer with each step we took, and then, as the coastline appeared to our left, we found a battalion of French soldiers, manning guns and facing east.

"Look!" said Mush, pointing into the distance.

He had spotted more Stukas, flying in from behind a ridge of low hills, along which were dotted German lines. They were less than ten kilometres away, far closer than I had feared.

"I told you," Mush added. "This is where we will die. There is no escape, brother."

I turned left, where a narrow street led down to the beaches. A huge number of troops simply idled about, and beyond them were even more men on the beach itself. Trapped, with their backs to the sea, and with no hope of breaking free, from the sky they must have resembled swarming ants.

"This can't be right," I said. "There must be a plan!"

Mush chuckled.

"When you discover a plan," he said, "let me know."

We went on for a hundred or so metres, before another air raid began. This time we ducked into a private residence – a three-storey town house missing its roof. I heard the Stukas long before they struck, and I wondered why they were still attacking the town. There was very little left to destroy. When I said this to Mush, he shook his head.

"You are naïve, Fazal," he replied. "They are following their orders, just as we are."

"But they are beyond cruel," I replied. "To kill women and children in such a way. It is inhumane. Have they no hearts? Can they not see the horrors they are unleashing?"

Since childhood, I had been taught to believe in human kindness and goodness, but that belief was fading. I thought of Lieutenant Cummings, the man I'd spoken to in Cassel. How he'd been unsure of his faith. Was I heading the same way?

I got so caught up in my own thoughts, that the raid passed me by. When it ceased, the landscape around us had changed again, with more fires raging and yet more smoke and debris. We moved on slowly, past even greater casualties, until finally we reached a signpost for Malo-les-Bains. And, within five minutes, we'd reunited with Company 32, on the coastal road, alongside thousands of other troops.

With nothing else to do, we sat on the road and waited. Sergeant Buckingham walked up and down the lines, checking on us and issuing nonsensical orders about staying put and not causing a fuss. None of the men were complaining, even though we had every right to. And with nowhere to go, what else could we do but sit and wait? Buckingham seemed drunk again and took several swigs from a hip flask until it ran dry. He cursed and flung it aside, before muttering to himself.

Part of me had grown to hate the Sergeant, but I couldn't help remembering that his father had died at the Somme. Perhaps that explained his hatred and anger, and perhaps that gave him some semblance of an excuse for his behaviour. Each of us was frightened and weary, and each of us coped with our stresses in particular ways. It was not for me to judge my sergeant, but I could not help disliking him nonetheless. He had insulted my country, my culture and my honour one too many times.

Before us lay the open sea, grey and choppy and filling the air with saltiness. From the road, a wide bank led steeply down onto the narrow beach, also crammed with troops. I nudged Mush, who was sitting with his eyes closed, deep in thought.

"The beach is not very wide," I told him.

He opened his eyes and took in the scene.

"It's high tide," he told me. "The sea will retreat this evening, and the beach will widen then."

"Tides?"

Mush shook his head, like a slightly disappointed teacher.

"The sea moves in and out with the tides," he explained. "You must remember that from our journey to Marseille."

"No," I admitted. "I was too busy dreaming about what we might see in France. Or tending to the mules."

"You mean they didn't teach you about tides at your fancy school?" Mush added.

"No, they didn't," I replied.

"Hmm," he said. "You're very stupid for someone so clever."

"And you're very ugly," I joked. "We make a good team, brother!"

He punched my shoulder playfully, closed his eyes and went back to daydreaming. But not for very long. A shout went up, and then dive bombers appeared to the east. They sped along the coastline, homing in on our position like angry hornets in late summer. Sergeant Buckingham blew his whistle and we ran towards the town itself, desperate to avoid the attack.

The sands erupted with bombs and gunfire, as our troops tried to escape. Many were cut down where they sat, and others as they ran. Some charged into the sea, eager to escape death, but it did no good. The water did not prevent the bullets from hitting their mark. The Stukas made three passes, and each time, they took more lives, and then they were gone as quickly as they'd arrived.

Clouds of smoke and dust polluted the air, and the sand turned red where the casualties were greatest. Screaming and groaning filled my ears, then shouting and calls for medics. Two ambulances made their way towards us, but their progress was slow because the area around the road was jam-packed with angry and panicked men. A few of my comrades began to clear a path, but a gang of white soldiers grew angry and a fight broke out. Captain Morrow and two other officers rushed to calm things down, and in all of the madness, the wounded continued to suffer.

"It's every man for himself and no mistake," said a British private close by. "I bet those officers were enjoying a nice cuppa as we sat in the open."

"Stands to reason, don't it?" said another. "One rule for them, another for us. Blinkin' toffs!"

A few murmurs became shouts, and I thought the private and his friends might start a riot, but then Sergeant Buckingham fired his pistol into the air.

"CALM DOWN!" he screamed. "THAT'S AN ORDER!"

A senior British officer turned up with some French soldiers and appealed for calm, before asking for volunteers to help the wounded, and to dig defensive bunkers in the sand. Many of my fellow Indians stayed put, but I could not. I charged down to help, grateful for something to take my mind off our situation. And it was in the sand that Private Sid Smith found me again.

"Well, well," he grinned. "Private Khan – that's a turn up! How are you, lad?"

I shook his hand as I replied.

"I'm alive," I told him. "What else can I tell you?"

Sid's smile grew even wider.

"How about telling me this is a dream?" he said. "And we'll wake up in London, drinking tea and eating cheese sandwiches on a summer's day?"

"If only that could be true," I replied.

"You never know," said Sid, grabbing a shovel. "Now, what are we doing?"

14

Between the frequent raids, we dug mini defences out of the sand, piling it high on the east-facing side. These bulwarks allowed us to take cover, but they did not protect against direct hits. However, they were better than nothing, and when the fifth raid started, many of us hid behind our work and prayed. From the air, those left exposed made clearer targets, whereas those in cover could only be seen once the German pilots turned and passed in the opposite direction. By then, we had taken positions on the other side of our little sand walls. We played this game throughout the raid. I'm not sure if we took any fewer casualties, but we had to try something.

After the fifth raid, Sid pointed towards Dunkirk's main port and grinned.

"They're here!" he exclaimed.

I looked up to see three naval vessels drawing into the harbour. Huge British destroyers.

"We're being evacuated," he told me. "Going back to Blighty, lad!"

"But there are only three ships," I replied. "How can they take us all?"

"They're just the first," Sid told me. "The Navy will send more, I'm sure of it. Come on – let's get closer!"

I turned to see my company emerging from buildings along the main road and shook my head.

"I cannot," I replied. "I must stay with my own corps."

Sid shrugged.

"Do you think they'll miss you?" he asked. "In this chaos?"

"But I have a duty," I said. "*Hukum Hai*."

"*Hokum* bleedin' *what'um*?" he replied.

I repeated our motto and explained what it meant.

"Fair enough, lad," he told me. "But I doubt you'll be moving off anytime soon. There are tens of thousands of troops between us and those ships."

I shook my head.

"I'll be here," I told him. "If you come back."

Sid gave me his mischievous grin once again.

"Who knows mate?" he replied, before setting off. "Maybe I'll see you in London?"

*

Half an hour passed before the German planes returned. Although we took cover again, this time they ignored us and flew by. I watched them approach the port and my heart sank. They were aiming for the naval vessels. Several Stukas banked left and right, ready to flank the ships, as two larger Heinkels positioned themselves to fly directly overhead.

Suddenly, Allied troops began to appear on the coastal road, rolling huge 40mm Bofors anti-aircraft guns into position. They turned skywards and began to fire at the German planes. Even from a distance, the sound was deafening. Thud after thud, with the first salvo missing their targets completely. Then, a second wave, and this time, they found a target. One of the Stukas banked sharply before beginning to nosedive. Smoke poured from its tail, as it crashed into the sea and exploded.

"Take that!" yelled someone behind me.

The men started to whoop and cheer, but it was too soon to celebrate, as the German planes struck. Mini explosions lit up one of the destroyers, and then a larger blast rocked the ship's stern. On land, another bomb landed next to an oil tank and the whole thing was blown into the air. I watched in horror as a second direct hit took out some nearby trucks and an ambulance, and then the Stukas began to strafe the area.

They swooped in low as our gunners tried and failed to hit them. The Stukas found their range and let loose.

"NO!"

The destroyer began to tip backwards and hundreds of men waiting to board were forced to jump into the sea. Overhead, another swarm of German planes raced to engage. Only this time, as they passed overhead, they sprayed us with bullets too. The soldier nearest to me pitched forwards and fell dead to the sand. Another fell close by, and then another. I dived to the floor, praying that I might survive.

"Messerschmitts!" shouted someone else. "Coming in low!"

Beside me, a rifleman raised his Lee Enfield and began to take pot shots at the incoming fighters. Suddenly, another fifty or so men joined in. It seemed I was the only one without a weapon. I thought about crawling away but could not bring myself to leave the fight. Instead, I rolled over to a fallen comrade and took the gun still in his hands. I had never fired a Lee Enfield before but had learned to shoot in basic training. I lay back and mimicked the nearest Tommy, and soon I was taking pot shots too.

"Aim higher!" the man next to me shouted.

I did as he asked, but it made little difference. The fighters were too far away to sustain any lasting damage from our .303 cartridges. Nonetheless, we continued until the immediate danger had passed. Over by the port, however, the attack continued.

"ALL ARMED PERSONNEL TO PORT!" a senior officer ordered. "DEFEND THE PORT!"

The soldiers around me began to rush towards the chaos, but I stayed put and dropped my rifle. As a member of the service corps, I had not been given a weapon, and was not allowed to use one without permission. It made little sense in our situation, with guns lying all about us and an armed enemy to fight. I longed to join in but thought better of it. I had already broken the rules by firing at the Messerschmitts. As ridiculous as it seemed in war, if Sergeant Buckingham caught me with a weapon, I'd be in serious trouble.

I ran towards the road instead, eager to get off the beach. And when I turned to survey the scene, I saw thousands of soldiers caught in the water around the docks, and thousands more pressing towards it. Allied troops were packed onto the beaches and surrounding area, for as far as the eye could see. And above them, the German onslaught continued, with more planes joining the attack until there were twenty-five in all.

I decided to seek out my company but could not see them anywhere. There were too many people, all moving in opposing directions, with no one sure of what to do next. I got caught in the flow, pushed this way and that, and tried to not to stumble and get trampled underfoot. Suddenly Mush grabbed my arm and hauled me aside, and I gasped for air.

"What are you doing?" he shouted. "Have you lost your mind?"

"I got caught up," I explained. "After I helped with the defences."

Mush clapped me around the ear.

"I told you to leave them to it," he said. "What use are we without weapons? Just stay out of trouble, Fazal. This is their war, brother. Let them fight it."

"No!" I said. "I will defend myself and my comrades."

"If they wanted us to fight," said Mush, "they would have armed us! Instead, we stand around like goats awaiting a pack of wolves."

I searched the area for more of my company but did not see anyone.

"Where's everyone else?" I asked.

"Taking cover," said Mush. "Just like we should be doing."

He grabbed my arm and dragged me away, as behind us another huge blast rocked the docks.

15

Calm descended as dusk fell. I sat on a hotel lobby floor, my back to a wall. I had been dozing, drifting in and out of a recurrent dream. I'd been back in my village, just south of Rawalpindi, herding water buffalo towards a drinking hole. Despite my not being one, in the dream, I had become a farmer's son. The sun was high, and lunchtime was upon us, but I still had many tasks to complete. I was thirsty and hungry, and longed for some shade.

The buffalo moved as one, each leading the other, drawn to the water's edge. They called out and jostled for position but worked as a team. Each knew every other's role and they were all able to take a drink. As I watched them, my grandfather approached me. Only he was younger and looked more like my father. He sat beside me and offered me tea, and I was confused because there was no tea.

"You can survive anything, as long as you have a cup of tea," he told me.

"I don't understand," I replied.

"Of course not," he said. "Now, on the way back, we need to be ruthless with these dumb animals."

"Ruthless?"

My grandfather nodded.

"There's not enough for all of them," he told me.

"Enough of what?" I asked.

"Stop talking," he said, producing a cup of tea and sipping from it.

I looked around but could not work out where the tea had come from.

"You must pay attention, my son. Orders are orders."

"But..."

"You see the large ones?" he said, pointing towards the herd. "They are useful. We will allow them."

"Baba, please!" I replied. "You're not making sense."

"Listen!" he snapped. "Pick out the weakest. They are useless. We cannot take them."

"But they are part of the herd," I said. "Each buffalo has a role to play."

My grandfather looked to the west and shook his head.

"No," he replied. "Not today. There's a storm coming, Fazal, and we must save ourselves."

I turned to the west but saw nothing on the horizon, and my grandfather slurped irritatingly at his tea – something he abhorred in others.

"But, where is the storm?" I asked.

He cupped an ear and cocked his head to one side.

"Listen. . ." he told me. "You can hear them. . ."

Almost immediately, the buzzing began. A black cloud appeared in the distance. It drew near at astonishing speed, and I saw that it was made up of hornets. Thousands and thousands of angry hornets. I sprang to my feet and rushed towards the water, but my grandfather did not follow. Instead, he sat there and began to laugh.

"No point rushing into the water," he shouted, as the hornets swarmed all around him. "The water cannot save you. . ."

I awoke with a start, my entire body drenched in sweat, and cried out,

"They're coming!"

A few of the men stirred, but none woke up. Night had fallen, and apart from occasional voices from outside, there was a welcome and surprising hush. The darkness protected us from further German air raids and gave us time to rest. I stood carefully, trying not to disturb anyone, and made my way outside, stepping over countless sleeping men. Trying to forget my dream.

On the beaches, it was chilly and breezy. I saw the

light of many small fires and men huddled together to keep warm. I wondered if the Germans saw them too, as they waited outside Dunkirk, ready to strike at sunrise. I heard a few shouts of "put them out" but saw very little adherence to that order. Like me, many of the troops seemed resigned to Fate. We would either make it onto a ship and be rescued or die in the attempt. Those were our only options.

I decided to take a walk, my dream still resonating, and tried to work out what my grandfather had been telling me. But the more I considered it, the less I could comprehend. As I turned off the coastal road, I saw a group of women huddled next to an ambulance. They were nurses, and when they saw me approaching, they smiled.

"Get some rest, Private," said one of them.

She was tall, with brown hair tied in a bun and wrinkles around her eyes and mouth. Her expression was friendly and warm, and she seemed to be a similar age to my mother. She held a tin cup of tea in one hand and a cigarette in the other.

"I cannot sleep," I told her. "Bad dreams."

"Seems silly doesn't it?" she replied. "That in the midst of this waking nightmare, we can still have bad dreams. You'd think the human imagination could not dream up worse than this."

"You would," I told her. "I am Fazal Khan, Company 32, Royal Indian Army Service Corps."

The woman held out a hand.

"Lillian," she said. "Nurse. Your English is very good."

"I learned at school," I told her. "In Punjab."

A cloud passed across her face – perhaps some sad memory – and then she smiled again.

"I knew a boy from Punjab once," she said. "He was a Sikh. But that was many years ago, when I was a young nurse. He was brought to Brighton Pavilion during 1915. There were many injured Indians there."

"My grandfather also," I told her. "He was injured at the Somme."

"A ghastly business," she replied. "We thought it could never happen again, and yet here we are."

"I do not understand this war," I admitted. "Why one empire fights another, when both look the same."

Nurse Lillian shook her head.

"Me neither," she replied. "But that is not our concern, Fazal. We are only pawns in their game and must obey."

The other three nurses began to drain their cups and stub out their cigarettes. When Lillian saw them, she sighed.

"Back to work," she told me. "No rest for the wicked and all that."

"This boy," I asked, "that you knew in Brighton?"

Lillian shrugged.

"Oh," she said. "He died, I think. I lost contact with him."

"You remember him, however?"

Lillian nodded.

"He was hard to forget," she told me. "But enough of that. See you around, Private Khan. Or perhaps not, hey?"

"I do not understand."

Lillian sighed.

"I'm a nurse, son," she explained. "If I see you again, you'll probably be injured or worse."

"Ah," I said. "How silly of me."

I walked around in circles for some time, until dawn began to break across the eastern horizon. I had not prayed for some while, so I decided to read *Fujr*, which is the morning prayer. I strolled down to the sea and began to wash my face, arms, hands and feet. The salty water was cold and gave me a shock, but I did not stop. Although my uniform was unclean, I decided to continue. In any other circumstance, dirty clothes for prayer were forbidden. But I could not afford to become fussy. And I needed the solemnity and reassurance that praying would bring.

Turning to the east, I raised my hands to my shoulders, palms flat and facing outwards, and began to pray.

16

On my return to the damaged hotel, I found Mush and Sadiq drinking tea outside. Their uniforms were as crumpled as mine, and both looked dreadful – exhausted and disillusioned.

"Where did that come from?" I asked.

"Captain Ashdown," said Sadiq. "I'm surprised you were not first in line."

I ignored his jibe, turning to Mush instead.

"Any news on our departure?"

Mush shrugged.

"Nothing but tea and a few bars of chocolate," he replied. "Here, I saved you some."

He handed me three small bars of chocolate and a cup. I ate first, polishing off two bars in an instant, before taking my time drinking. The tea was warm and sugary, and very comforting. It added to my mood, already calmed by my walk and my prayer.

"I'm not sure we can stand another assault like yesterday," said Mush. "We were lucky."

"Did we lose any men?"

Mush shook his head.

"That's what I meant by lucky," he told me. "It is a miracle."

Captain Ashdown stood by the bank that led down to the sand, using field glasses to view the port area. The sunken destroyer blocked one part of the harbour, but the other two had returned and been joined by several smaller vessels. The troops were streaming towards the dock once more, and even without help, I could see that the evacuation continued. It was only a matter of time before the Germans resumed their attack.

As Captain Morrow joined Ashdown, I made my way towards them, through the massed ranks of Company 32. Ushering greetings to several comrades, I was asked all sorts of questions. Having no answers for any of them, I passed by quickly with a few shrugs and shakes of the head.

"You must know something?" said one of them, about twenty yards from where the captain stood.

"No, friend," I told the man. "There have been no orders yet. Have patience."

"How can I be patient?" the man asked me. "We have waited and waited for news."

I didn't know what to say, and as I walked away, the officers made their way down to the sand and began a guarded conversation. I got as close as possible, shielded by other men heading towards the port and a disabled supply truck. And, despite the crowds, I managed to hear some of their conversation.

"I will not leave these men behind," said Captain Ashdown.

"But the orders are clear," Captain Morrow replied. "We cannot disobey them."

Captain Ashdown was enraged, his face red and expression stern.

"These men have been loyal servants since India," he said. "Imagine the impact our betrayal will have over there. We brought them here in good faith. We cannot leave them to the Germans. That would be immoral!"

My heart sank as he spoke, and I realised why we had been left sitting around: command had told Captain Ashdown to leave us behind.

"They are not front-line personnel!" Captain Morrow continued. "For God's sake, John, they aren't even armed!"

"They supply the lines," Captain Ashdown retaliated. "They keep the combat troops armed and fed. It was bad enough leaving behind the mules. I will not allow this!"

Captain Morrow took Ashdown's arm.

"Look," he added. "I agree with you. But we cannot disobey an order. The consequences will be grave. I have to think of my career."

"Then you may turn away," Captain Ashdown told him. "Blame it on me. What good is my career with these poor souls on my conscience?"

"I cannot be a part of this," Morrow told him.

"Fine," said Captain Ashdown. "When the top brass holds us to account, I will shoulder the blame."

Captain Morrow nodded and walked away. As he did so, I returned to Mush and Sadiq, my heart heavy with anger and sadness. How could they contemplate abandoning us? We were four hundred souls. Four hundred sons and husbands, and fathers and brothers. We had come halfway across the Earth to help them, to serve a country and King that had yoked our people. Without a murmur of public protest, we had taken their orders and their insults, and survived the harshest of conditions, and for what? To be cast aside like worthless animals. Like the poor mules we'd left before entering Dunkirk.

Is that all we were worth to them? Is that all we meant? My mind raced, and my heart pounded faster, and I considered what I should do next. I wanted to run and hide and leave the madness of the evacuation behind. I felt ashamed and embarrassed of my desire to join up, my zeal in serving the British Army, my pride in our now meaningless motto.

"*Hukum Hai?*" I whispered to myself. "What about your duty to us, you scoundrels!"

"What is wrong?" Mush asked me.

I looked into his eyes, and the rage inside me turned to tears.

"Dear brother," he said. "Whatever has happened to you?"

I took him aside.

"Walk with me," I said. "I have news."

We wandered away, back into the broken and battered hotel. A beam had fallen through the lobby, crushing the front desk. The walls were charred from fire damage and smoke, and the stairwell blocked by fallen masonry and wood. Evidence of our shelter lay all around – chocolate wrappers, bandages browned with dirt and dried blood, and the smell of a hundred unwashed and weary men huddled together in a space built for a third of that number.

"They want to leave us behind," I eventually said.

"Who?"

"The people in charge."

I knew the ranks of these men in command. I could even picture them, in their medal-laden, pristine uniforms, with impeccable manners and cups of tea. Yet, I could not imagine how such cultured and educated beings could have so little heart and so few morals. I had met starving beggars with more generous hearts.

"How can you know this?" a shocked Mush asked me. "This is impossible!"

I shook my head.

"No," I replied. "I am certain. Captain Ashdown has refused to follow his orders. Captain Morrow and he were arguing on the beach. I eavesdropped on their conversation. There is no mistake."

"But..."

Mush was shaken. His face grew paler and he struggled to find words. We stood silently for a while, before he spoke again.

"Those treacherous dogs!" he growled. "I want to tear them apart!"

"But we can't," I said. "We can't do anything. We will have to trust in Captain Ashdown. He is a good man."

Mush snorted.

"One good man in a nest of a thousand snakes!"

"There are plenty more good people amongst them," I replied.

"*Pah!*" he said. "Imagine a choice between us and

their own people. Imagine us trying to board a ship, taking the place of the white people behind us. Would they be so welcoming then?"

"Perhaps some of them," I replied.

"We have been given our answer, Fazal," said Mush. "We have been shown our true worth. So, tell me, why should we continue to listen to their orders and do their bidding?"

"Because Captain Ashdown will save us," I replied. "And, as of this moment, he is our only hope. Without him, we will be left to the Germans."

Mush did not seem convinced.

"What choice do we have?" I added. "It's either evacuation to England or capture and possible death."

I was right, and that realisation hurt both of us. My faith in my role had been torn to shreds. My trust in the kindness and decency of others ended. It seemed I had reached a point of no return.

17

That day brought almost continuous German bombardment. From nine in the morning, until dusk fell just after seven, their campaign was merciless and relentless. Perhaps a hundred planes took part in the raids, in intervals of twenty minutes, exhausting and almost breaking the will of our forces. Or perhaps I would be better saying *their* forces, for the divide between British and Indian had been made clear to us. Our lowly rank absolutely undeniable. By day's end, everything had changed. Nothing would ever be the same again.

"Where the *hell* is the RAF?" Captain Morrow yelled, as the second wave of German planes appeared on the horizon.

"They must be tied up," Sergeant Buckingham replied. "There can be no other explanation."

"*Tied up?*" asked Sergeant Davis. "What in God's name is more important than this?"

The officers had gathered next to a mound of rubble that had once been a seafront café. Only one wall remained, the rest blown apart by a bomb. Captain Morrow held a map and pointed to parts of it.

I was openly listening to every word, no longer concerned about being seen. No longer concerned about their opinion of me. However, the officers paid me no mind, perhaps because the area was so crowded. Perhaps because, like me, they no longer cared either.

"The Germans have sunk a destroyer here," said Captain Morrow, tapping the map that flapped about on the wind. "The wreckage has blocked access into the harbour at this point."

"Meaning fewer ships can reach the docks," said Sergeant Davis. "So fewer men can be saved."

"They must have a contingency," Sergeant Buckingham replied. "After all, they must have assumed the Germans would attack. We're sitting ducks."

Captain Morrow shook his head.

"I've given up second guessing Command," he told them. "It's utterly pointless."

"What about the Indians?" Buckingham added. "Has Captain Ashdown seen sense yet?"

"No," said Captain Morrow. "And I doubt he'll change his mind."

Sergeant Buckingham sneered.

"Must be rather confusing," he said. "Being English and growing up over there. He's forgotten which side he's on."

"Enough!" said Morrow. "You may keep your opinions to yourself, Buckingham. I will not listen to them. John Ashdown is a fine soldier and one of the most loyal you will ever find. Do not insult him!"

"Sir!" said Buckingham, his face flushed with humiliation.

"And it's not *over there*, as you put it," Morrow added. "India is part of our Empire and we are sworn to defend it. Those men are with us."

A wave of Stukas appeared from the south, banking towards the port, but letting loose a few bullets as they passed us. Diving for cover, I caught my knee against some rubble and winced in pain. When the Stukas had passed, I sat up to find Sergeant Davis lying dead.

"GET A MEDIC!" Captain Morrow pointlessly screamed.

There was no saving the sergeant, but a passing ambulance stopped anyway, and a couple of nurses jumped out. They tended to Davis, but not for very long.

"This man is deceased," said one of them. "We'll

have to cover him up. There's nowhere to take the dead."

"Dear God!" said Captain Morrow. "Those blasted Germans!"

Captain Ashdown rushed towards us from the beach, holding his cap.

"Morrow?" he called out.

"It's Davis," said Captain Morrow. "He's had it, I'm afraid."

Captain Ashdown knelt beside his fallen comrade and seemed to say a prayer, or perhaps whisper something in remembrance. I couldn't be sure because a bomb exploded about a hundred yards away, leaving a massive crater on the beach.

"ATTACK!" yelled Captain Ashdown, jumping to his feet and blowing his whistle.

I hobbled towards the destroyed buildings, hoping to find some shelter, as a second wave of Stukas strafed us. Several bullets ripped into the side of the ambulance and I heard screaming.

"No!" I yelled, rushing to help, despite the danger.

The back of the truck was open, and I clambered aboard. The nurse who'd seen to Davis had been hit three times and was in a terrible state. The other younger nurse fought to find words over her shock.

"S. . .she. . .she. . ."

"Tend to her," I said. "I will check on the driver."

Climbing out again, I opened the driver's door and he fell out on top of me. I pushed him aside with help from a British soldier.

"Can you drive?" I asked him.

"Pardon?" he asked over another wave of explosions and gunfire.

"Drive?" I shouted. "Can you operate this truck?"

The man nodded.

"We need to get it to cover," I said. "Over to where the nurses are stationed. We cannot lose it!"

I jumped in, the other man beside me, and together we took the ambulance away from danger. Earlier that morning, whilst on my walk, I had found a field hospital, tucked away down a sheltered lane in Malo-les-Bains. I directed the driver towards it. But since my earlier sojourn, part of the route had been blocked by a fallen building and we had to find an alternative, under fire most of the way. The Germans seemed to have redoubled their efforts overnight.

Finally, after taking several more bullets, we edged into the medical zone, where the staff rushed about trying to save as many lives as possible. I jumped out and ran around the back, ignoring my gashed leg, and found the younger nurse crying.

"She died!" the woman wailed. "I tried, honest I did, but it were no use!"

As she wailed, and the driver joined me, I heard a familiar voice.

"Private Khan," said Lillian. "Changed jobs, have you?"

I turned to her and tried to smile, but there was no humour to be found.

"They were hit on the seafront," I said. "I'm afraid that one of your colleagues has died."

Lilian's face fell.

"I thought we should bring the ambulance to safety," I added. "It would do no good to lose another. We will need it."

Lillian nodded.

"Thank you both," she said. "But there is no shelter here. Nowhere is safe from these monsters, I'm afraid."

The driver left us, eager to return to his mates, and I sat on the truck's step and watched as the people around me tried to do their jobs. Lillian held out her hand.

"Come on, son," she said. "I'll find you some tea."

A smattering of bullets ripped into a wall not ten yards away.

"If we're not killed first," Lillian added. "Sometimes, I wonder if that might be best for all."

I nodded and followed her.

132

"But then," said Lillian, "I remember the pier at Brighton, and tea and stilton cheese, and I think it would be better to live."

I thought of my dream, and my grandfather's view that everything was fine, as long as you had tea.

"Tea would be most welcome," I said.

18

A while later, as I was about to return to the seafront, Captain Ashdown appeared, carrying a man over his shoulder. He looked worn out, as he laid the man down and tried to catch his breath. When he spotted me, he seemed unconcerned at my presence, merely nodding in my direction.

"Injured?" asked Lillian.

Captain Ashdown shook his head. His cheeks were scarlet from his exertions.

"Deceased," he replied.

It was Sergeant Davis' body, wrapped in ragged tarpaulin, but with care and affection.

"I could not leave him there," he told us. "Do you have a medical officer here?"

Lillian nodded. Her hair had come loose on the right side and hung over her ear.

"Two," she said. "You'd like them to record his death?"

"Yes," said my Captain. "He's an officer, nurse. I'd like to afford him some dignity if possible."

Lillian sighed and wiped her hands against her blood-spattered uniform.

"There's no dignity here," she said. "And we have no storage for the dead. I'm afraid it's all rather improper, regardless of one's status or rank."

They stared at each other for a moment, and tension filled the space between them. Then Lillian smiled and the skin around her dark eyes creased.

"Would you like some tea, Captain?"

"Ashdown," he replied. "And yes, please."

He turned to me.

"Khan?" he enquired.

"Do you know our brave private?" Lillian asked.

"Yes," said the Captain. "And I'm wondering why he's here."

"I helped to save an ambulance, sir," I told him. "It had been strafed with bullets."

"He also saved a nurse's life, Captain," Lillian added. "We could have lost two colleagues, were it not for Fazal Khan. I asked him to stay for some tea."

"I see," said Captain Ashdown. "Well done, Khan."

I waited for him to send me back, but the order did

not come. Instead, he sat on an upturned oil drum and bowed his head. Lillian went to a hastily erected mess tent, to fetch tea.

"Sir?" I asked.

"Yes, Khan?"

"Permission to. . ."

"Just speak, Private," he told me, his tone revealing exasperation. "There's no time for that nonsense now. Forget protocol!"

"I *know*," I told him. "I heard you talking. . ."

"Know about what?" he asked.

"The order to leave us behind," I said.

Chaos reigned all around us, yet at that moment, we could have been the only people there. Captain Ashdown's face fell, and he shook his head.

"I see," he said. "And you heard my feelings on the subject?"

I nodded.

"That is why I am speaking to you," I told him. "You are the only one I can trust."

"No, no," said the Captain. "The others are good men. They're just following orders, trying to cope with the lunacy of this mission."

"No," I replied. "Sergeant Buckingham hates us, and the others see us as beasts of burden, just like our poor mules. You are the only one who cares for us."

Captain Ashdown was about to reply, when Lillian returned with two cups.

"I brought you some more," she told me. "I hope there's nothing urgent for you to return to."

The captain scoffed.

"That's exactly the point," he told us. "There will be no more orders. I've been told to get as many men onto ships as I can, as soon as I can. Failing that, I should save myself. . ."

"You've explicitly been told this?" asked Lillian.

"As good as," he replied. "It's every man for himself from now on."

Lillian coughed.

"I'm sorry," said Captain Ashdown. "Women, too."

"I think you'll find we women stick together, regardless," she told him. "It's the job, Captain. I thought you chaps were the same."

"We are," I replied, eager to defend my captain and my company. "But the situation is not of our making."

"Pawns," Lillian repeated from earlier that morning. "That is all we are. Pushed around some imaginary games board, whilst our masters drink brandy and make bombastic speeches to deceive those at home."

Captain Ashdown's shock was undisguised.

"How can you think such things?" he asked.

Lillian shrugged.

"Precisely because I *can* think for myself," she replied. "Look around you, Captain. Who dies in these wars? Can you see an emperor, a prime minister or a chancellor here?"

"You're a communist!" said Captain Ashdown.

"Not quite," Lillian told him. "I am just a weary and disillusioned woman whose son is missing in action – a son whose father also disappeared after the Great War – and whose uncle was shamed and imprisoned because he defied polite society and fell in love."

"But what of serving our country, our—"

"You mean as I have done?" I asked, anxious that I hadn't overstepped the mark. "I have chosen to serve and yet I am to be cut loose, like my animals before me."

When Lillian showed puzzlement, I explained what had been decided, and she grew enraged.

"That is utterly despicable!" she snapped at the Captain. "How can you allow this, sir?"

He shook his head.

"I cannot allow it," he replied. "I will not allow it. It is morally wrong."

Lillian nodded and placed a hand on his.

"Surely, you will be punished for disregarding an order," she said.

"I should imagine so," said the Captain, seemingly

resigned to his fate.

"Punished for doing the morally decent thing," she replied. "And you wonder why I am so disillusioned?"

He shrugged and looked at me.

"You realise we need to keep this from the men?" he said. "It will be difficult to control them should word get out."

"It is already too late for that," I told him. "But they *will* follow you, sir. If you explain yourself..."

As Captain Ashdown stared off into the distance, lost in his own thoughts, Lillian and I chatted a while longer. Eventually, a fresh wave of German fighter planes cut us short.

"Good luck," she said to us, as we left.

"Thank you, madam," I told her.

"Oh, Private Khan!" she replied with a smile. "I do hate being called madam. Lillian will do."

"Lillian," I repeated.

"And *Captain*?" she added.

"Yes, Miss?" he said, turning to face her.

"You are doing the right thing by these men," she told him. "No matter what the outcome, do not forget that. Honour and duty are not always bound together. Sometimes, the most noble course of action is also the least welcome."

19

On our return to the seafront, the rest of Company 32 were hanging around, taking cover when required, and generally restless. Captain Ashdown told me he wanted to bring the men together, but in the chaos, that would prove impossible. The area around the beaches had grown even busier, and to the west, the port of Dunkirk was ablaze. Several naval ships were stationed out at sea, and I could see a line of boats leading to one of them. Hundreds of soldiers made their way out, and many more stood on the beach, awaiting their own evacuation.

North of the port, and closest to us, a few smaller ships bobbed in the water, just past a mile-long concrete and wood jetty. The ships did not come any closer, and I guessed that the water was too shallow to allow it. Instead, they began dropping rowing boats and dinghies into the sea. A number of men waded out towards them, eager to get aboard, and once those on the beach realised, a great stampede began, with people being knocked over and trampled underfoot. Captain Ashdown had said it was every man for themselves, and now I saw it with my own eyes.

"Why don't they show some discipline?" I asked.

"Because they have lost all sense of it," Mush told me. "This is it, now. No more orders."

As the day before, there was no one taking charge of the effort. Senior officers were around, but not one tried to organise the troops, or lead the evacuation. No one seemed to care any more. A general sense of apathy had tainted us all. So much so, that even the air raids seemed less frightening, and more of a nuisance. I'd heard and witnessed so many explosions, so many deaths and injuries, that I didn't even feel scared.

Life or death were in the hands of Luck. As the Stukas peppered us with bullets and incendiaries, and the Heinkels dropped larger bombs, survival sat between simple lines. If you were within close proximity of a strike, you would probably be injured or killed. If you were lucky, and they missed your position, you lived. You could run or stand still, walk or crawl, take cover or not. None of it made a bit of difference. Chance was all you had. My mother had once told me that your life and death were written before you began your journey.

"When your time comes," she'd said, "you cannot escape Fate."

That fatalism, that many British thought applied only to the Indians, had now become their attitude too. On the beach, I saw British troops sitting in circles, playing cards and drinking tea, if they had any left. They made sandcastles with their hands and several were kicking a leather ball around. Many lay on their backs, taking in the air or snoozing as they waited for whatever came next, or they sat and laughed and joked with their friends and comrades. If not for the bombs and dead bodies, it could have been a scene from some bizarre military holiday.

"Khan!" Captain Ashdown shouted.

"Yes, sir!" I replied, approaching him.

He took me aside.

"We need to move quickly," he explained. "The longer we leave it, the more chance of missing out. If word gets out about leaving you chaps behind, people may try to stop us."

I smiled at his use of *us*. It rebuilt a little of the faith I had lost. However, organising the men would be almost unmanageable.

"How can we get them together?" I asked.

"Call the men," said the captain. "But make the call in Punjabi. That way, they will understand, and the English speakers won't. Get Private Ahmad to help you and anyone else you can trust. We'll rendezvous over there."

He pointed to a narrow lane that led from the coastal road, back into town. A half-destroyed clothing shop stood alone in the rubble of its former neighbours. A small battalion of battered and drained French soldiers trudged past it, heading for the port, too.

"Sir!" I said.

I rushed to find Mush, suddenly re-energised at the thought of evacuation. It did not take me long. My friend was lecturing a group of our comrades, stabbing at the air with an index finger to make his point.

"It's time, Mush!" I yelled in Punjabi. "Gather the men!"

He looked confused, so I pointed at our rendezvous.

"Captain Ashdown's orders," I said, sticking to our mother tongue. "We must act quickly, before the others try to stop us."

"We are leaving?"

"Yes!" I told him. "But only if we hurry. Help me tell the men and speak only in Punjabi. The British cannot know what we are planning!"

Mush nodded.

"So, the captain is willing to risk his medals for us?"

"I told you he was!" I replied. "We must trust him. Now, move!"

I grabbed a couple of other men. They already knew of our betrayal and were eager to help once I explained what was happening. Once they realised there was still hope.

"Inshallah!" one of them exclaimed. "*Allah Rakka Ashdown-ji!*"

His words meant "God Keep Captain Ashdown Safe" and became a little chorus. As Mush and the others gathered our company, I rushed away to find more of my comrades, and within half an hour, we were gathered at our meeting point.

Captains Ashdown and Morrow awaited us, alongside a miserable Sergeant Buckingham. His stubble had grown through want of shaving and deep dark circles had formed around his eyes. He stood behind his seniors and paid little attention to what Captain Ashdown was saying.

"Right, men!" the captain shouted. "I must be brief – no time to lose! I'm sure most of you have heard rumours about being left behind—"

A few groans and shouts interrupted him, and he held up his hand.

"Let me be very clear," he continued. "I will not leave a single living man behind."

A huge cheer drew the attention of those round about us. Captain Ashdown realised and hurried to complete his address.

"We move now," he said. "And quickly. I will go ahead with Captain Morrow and a few others, to find us a berth. The rest of you will follow, in groups of ten. Each of you is responsible for the other. Is that clear?"

The men nodded and shouted in approval.

"No man will be left behind unless they are killed. We cannot take the dead, and you are forbidden from carrying them. The injured will be your responsibility – each team to carry their own. We will show dignity and unity, and extreme discipline. Understood?"

Another roar of approval.

"If you get left behind, I cannot help you," he added. "You will have to find your way onto a ship. But we must not let that happen. *Hukum Hai*, gentlemen!"

The troops looked at each other and then cheered.

"*HUKUM HAI! HUKUM HAI!*" they chanted.

I turned to Mush, who was grinning.

"At last!" he said. "Let's go!"

I watched Sergeant Buckingham's face explode with rage. He whispered to Captain Morrow, continually shaking his head. When Morrow replied, Buckingham threw his hands in the air, utterly disgusted.

"Stuff that!" I heard him shout.

He turned and walked away, and Captain Morrow shouted after him.

"Come back, Sergeant. That is an order!"

Buckingham turned and smiled.

"Court martial me," he declared. "I *dare* you!"

He went on his way, and I worried that he might cause us trouble down the line. "Hopefully," I said to Mush, "we'll never see him again."

"Good riddance," Mush replied.

"Right, men!" Captain Ashdown yelled. "This is it. Move out!"

My heart thudded, and my stomach flipped. Whatever was coming, I prayed that we would survive it.

20

Captain Ashdown called me to him.

"You're to come with me, Khan," he said. "Bring Private Ahmad too. I need you to act as messengers. Once we know we have a ship, you'll guide the men towards it. Clear?"

I nodded as Mush pulled a face, so Captain Ashdown explained in Punjabi.

"Okay," he said in English. "All good, sir!"

The captain nodded.

"Come on," he said. "There's much to get done."

We made our way along the road, as the going was easier than by beach. Ahead of us lay a canal that surrounded the port, but we did not need to cross it. Out destination was the long jetty, and the boats close by it. By now, the number of boats had grown, and some of them were small enough to come closer to the beach. One, a decrepit old tugboat seemed to be grounded. The crew were abandoning ship and wading towards the beach. Fifty or so men passed them in the opposite direction, and when they reached the tug, they boarded it.

"It won't go anywhere," Mush told me. "It is completely stuck."

A sudden air attack made us flatten ourselves against a wall, as the hundreds of men around us ducked. Four Stukas peppered the area with bullets and hit numerous targets, before a small bomb landed on the beached tugboat. It exploded into flame, and I heard the screams of burning men and looked away, only to see more devastation ahead.

Three large bombs landed close together around the port. Huge torrents of water, maybe forty feet high, exploded into the air and lethal debris flew in all directions. A section of the docks creaked and groaned, and then fell away, landing on the desperate men in the water below.

"Move on!" Captain Morrow ordered. "We must keep going!"

We got to within a quarter-mile of the jetty, when the situation grew even worse. Within seconds the skies seemed to darken with German planes – Heinkels, Messerschmitts and those dreaded Stukas with their awful whining. They concentrated on the section of beach nearest the port, where the largest mass of troops had gathered, wading out to sea and waiting to be recused. Bomb after bomb fell on those poor souls, and yet they continued to push on, whether through hope or resignation. It was hard to tell. I turned to Captain Ashdown.

"We cannot board from there, sir," I told him. "There are too many already waiting."

"Noted, Khan," he replied.

He held up his hand.

"Rest a moment," he said. "Morrow, any ideas?"

Captain Morrow surveyed the scene and did not speak for a while.

"We could try praying, John," he joked. "There's nothing else to do."

The largest vessels were a mile out to sea and could not come any closer. The smaller boats and dinghies were being crowded by the men already in the water. With no other way out to the rescue boats, we were stuck again.

"There has to be a way!" said Captain Ashdown.

I looked east for some reason, away from our intended destination, and saw something amazing happening. A few hundred yards away, some of the men were driving or pushing abandoned and partially-destroyed vehicles towards the water. The first in line drove into the sea and continued until his supply truck was submerged up to its doors. Then, he jumped out and called more men to him. Together, they pushed the vehicle further and further until only its roof could be seen. The driver clambered on top and began to wave his arms.

A second truck was manoeuvred in the same fashion, and then a third, much taller supply truck passed them, before it too was pushed into the line by ten soldiers, with an eleventh on the roof until he was half-submerged himself.

"A gangway!" I shouted. "They're using vehicles to build a gangway!"

"Whatever are you. . .?" began Captain Ashdown, only for the sight to leave his speechless.

"Good God!" said Captain Morrow. "That's ingenious!"

"We must help," I told them. "We would gain their trust and they might help us too."

Captain Ashdown nodded.

"You might just be right, Khan," he said, giving me a warm smile. "Come along!"

We ran towards the men, and when they saw two captains, they saluted and pointed back towards the road, where countless vehicles had been left under fire.

"If it drives, bring it here," said one of the men,

whose front teeth were missing. "Even if it's falling apart. It all helps!"

"Anything that don't move, grab some men and get them to push it along," said another.

"But we'll never create a mile-long jetty," said Captain Morrow.

"We don't need to, sir," said the second man. "We just need the larger vessels to spot us and send rowing boats and dinghies our way. They're too busy concentrating on the port area to see us. We need to attract their attention."

"The coastal shelf here is very gradual," Captain Ashdown added. "We should be able to get at least halfway, with enough help."

"But the tallest vehicle is already under water," Captain Morrow pointed out.

"No problem, sir," said the second man. "We'll collect tables and oil drums, planks and supply boxes and the like. Anything we can use to create a platform on top of the vehicles. That'll raise us high enough."

Captain Ashdown glanced at Captain Morrow.

"It's worth a shot," he said.

"Absolutely."

Morrow turned to me.

"Redirect the men this way – all haste!"

I nodded, then Mush and I went to carry out his order.

"Bring any drivers first and see if you can gather some British chaps too – the more, the merrier!"

"Yes, sir!" I yelled.

We worked for a few hours, through the continued German attack, and despite being cold and wet. By the time we stopped, over two hundred men lay exhausted on the sand, and another three hundred stood on the makeshift jetty or in the water around it. Further along, others had seen what was happening and begun their own impromptu piers.

"Terribly clever idea, Private," said Captain Ashdown, as we stood resting at the water's edge. "Well done."

"Name's Cooper, sir," said the second man from earlier. "Vince to me mates."

He was short and stocky with wide shoulders and strong hands. His uniform was torn and shabby, and his boots had holes in them.

"Well, Vince," Captain Ashdown replied. "I hope your seniors appreciate your ingenuity."

Private Cooper shrugged.

"We're on our own, sir," he replied. "Haven't seen an officer in two days. They told us to head for the beaches and get back to Blighty any way we could. There's me and twelve others. The rest are either missing or dead."

Captain Ashdown nodded.

"Well, we're here now, Private," he told him. "And protocol dictates that I assume command over you and your men. We can't have leaderless troops."

"Absolutely, sir!" said Cooper.

"I've got a full complement of four hundred Indian service corps with me," the Captain explained. "You and your fellows can join us."

Private Cooper nodded, then smiled at me.

"Private Fazal Khan," I said, holding out a hand which he shook. "RIASC."

"Vince," said Private Cooper. "No need for the formalities, my friend."

A German fly-past made us duck in unison.

"Crafty Germans!" said Vince. "You'd think they'd get bored and buzz off!"

"No chance of that," I replied. "Not until nightfall."

"Well," he said. "We'd better try and attract some attention. You ready to test out our jetty?"

I nodded and pulled Mush towards me.

"Private Ahmad," I said. "My best friend."

Vince and Mush shook hands, and then we clambered onto the makeshift jetty. One of Vince's comrades came too, carrying sticks onto which strips of tablecloth had been tied. They were chequered red and white, and fluttered in the breeze.

"Afternoon chaps!" said the man. He was a giant, at least six feet four, with thick black stubble and extremely hairy spade-like hands.

"This is Private Milligan," said Vince. "He's a bit of a hairy Herbert, but a good bloke with it."

A trident of Messerschmitts whizzed by overhead, and a few bullets creased the water barely ten feet away. We waited to see if they would return, but they moved on to bigger targets. Then, with a deep breath and a silent prayer, the four of us edged our way out.

21

We stood on our precarious construction for over an hour, waving our flags and shouting until we grew hoarse. But no little boats came. Behind us, many of the men had waded as far as they could and stood expectantly in the cold water. The officers were halfway across the makeshift jetty, sitting with their legs dangling into the sea.

On the beaches, the crowds were now so large, that many men simply stood in lines, facing the sea, but without any hope of rescue. Fires raged across the scene, from west of Dunkirk's port, all the way around and past us, and on towards the east. The sound of shelling and gunfire and explosions did not let up. And soon we began to see the occasional body bobbing on the water's surface, many having been burnt.

"They're concentrating attacks on the boats now," said Vince, before licking his lips.

The skin around his mouth had dried and begun to peel through dehydration. The paradox of being surrounded by water with none to drink made me think of Coleridge's poem, "Rime of the Ancient Mariner", which we had learned at school. I mouthed its most famous line and smiled a little.

"Don't look good," said Milligan. "We could be stuck here for days."

"It won't last that long," I told them. "The Germans can't be more than six miles out and they're getting closer every hour. If we don't get out soon, we'll be overrun."

I glanced back to see a bombed-out Bofors gun sitting on the seafront road, long since rendered useless. With so little firepower, we couldn't even fight back.

"If this goes belly up," said Vince, "it's over. Hitler and his boys will have conquered most of Western Europe."

"With the entire British Armed Forces in captivity," I added.

"And England next on his list," said Milligan.

"What a mess!" said Vince. "I thought we'd put up a better show than this."

"Me too," I told him.

"British have messed up the war," Mush added. "Idiot tactics!"

Vince glared at Mush for a second, before bursting into laughter.

"Too right, friend!" he said. "Shameful this is. Running home like scared children."

"If we escape," I said, just like many times before, "we can rebuild and fight back. Sometimes retreating is the only option."

"Won't win me any medals, though, will it?" said Milligan. "I always fancied me a Victoria Cross or some such thing."

"You'll be lucky to get a pint and a pork pie, lad," said Vince.

"What is a pint?" I asked.

"Beer, Private Khan," he said. "It's sold in pints back home. You must have beer in India."

"We do," I told him. "But I am not allowed to drink it."

"Not allowed?" asked Vince, looking aghast. "Who's stopping you?"

"God," I replied. "Alcohol is forbidden in my religion."

"Blimey" said Vince. "I'd change religion, mate! I love a nice pint of an evening."

I smiled.

"I am happy with my religion," I told him. "But, I hope you get your pint!"

"Twenty-two miles," said Vince. "That's all there is between us and home, and the nearest pub!"

Mush smirked.

"Not for us," he replied. "Thousands of miles for us."

Vince looked at Mush and then shrugged.

"Mate," he said. "If you're fighting with us against the Germans, you've as much right to call England home as anyone. I'd stand you a pint any old time."

"I am Muslim too," said Mush. "No beer."

"Blimey!" said Vince. "I'll stand you a pint of blinkin' water and a pork pie then!"

This time I burst into laughter.

"What?" asked Milligan.

"Pork is also forbidden," I explained, wiping away a tear and remembering something Sid Smith had said.

"Dear God!" said Vince. "Is that a religion or torture?"

"A cheese sandwich and some tea, perhaps?" I added, not taking offence at his joke.

Vince grinned.

"How very English," he joked.

I heard Captain Ashdown shouting.

"BOATS!" he yelled, holding up his field glasses. "BOATS ARE COMING!"

We peered at the near horizon and saw nothing, and

then suddenly, a rowing boat appeared, with a single man at the oars.

"At last!" said Vince.

"We're going home!" yelled Milligan, grabbing Mush in a bear hug and almost knocking them both into the water. "We're going home!!!"

A second boat appeared and then three dinghies, and before long there were ten small vessels closing in to our position. Behind us, Captain Ashdown began to organise the men, telling them to make their way towards us. Those in the water already waded further and began to climb onto the makeshift jetty. It rocked and wobbled a little but stayed strong. And finally, a naval vessel appeared – the source of the smaller boats. It flew a red flag and Vince identified it immediately.

"Merchant Navy," he told us. "Looks a good size, too!"

The wailing started to the south this time, quiet but ominous, and then louder and louder.

"WATCH OUT!" yelled Milligan, as the Stuka homed in and began to fire its machine guns. A second appeared behind it, before banking right so that they flew in parallel. I froze to the spot, watching the bullets zip across the water in our direction, and then three bombs, one after the another – *PUFT! PUFT! PUFT!* – in an almost perfectly straight line. What felt like a mountain of water erupted over us and then I was falling into the sea, screams all around me, perhaps mine, perhaps not.

I landed on my back with a slap, and then I was coughing and spluttering and trying to grab onto something. My left hand found the handle of a truck door, and I managed to pull myself towards it, and then above salty water, gasping for air. I clung on, desperate to find Mush and Vince and Milligan, but they were nowhere to be seen.

With my shock residing, I hauled myself up and out of the sea, and clambered onto the roof of the vehicle underneath me. Part of our construction had collapsed, but it was still standing, and when I looked, the boats were still coming. I crouched and took deep breaths and then began to call for my friends. Behind me, Captain Ashdown found his voice and called for the men to keep moving forwards.

"Get on the boats!" he yelled. "Move!"

I began to panic then, scared that my friends had been killed, but Mush appeared opposite me, and Vince with him. They were soaked and shocked, and glad to be alive.

"Where's Milligan?" Vince asked.

"I cannot find him," I replied. "He must be in the water."

162

We searched the area around the makeshift jetty but couldn't see Milligan's massive frame anywhere. As the first of the rowing boats neared us, Vince shook his head.

"I'm not leaving without him," he said, before calling call out his name. "Milligan! Milligan!"

I shook my head and looked at Mush.

"He is gone," Mush said in Punjabi.

22

As the rowing boat pulled alongside, I knelt and called out to the sailor.

"Private Khan, RIASC," I told him. "My captain is right behind us."

The young man looked surprised. He cannot have been much older than me. He wore a black tunic with a v-necked collar, black trousers and a matching round hat. His shirt was white, and his skin pink and rosy.

"You Indian?" he asked.

"Yes," I said. "Service Corps."

"Any others with you?"

I nodded.

"Four hundred of my comrades," I told him. "And two officers and a band of twelve or so Tommys."

"Blimey," the sailor replied. *"Four hundred?* That's going to take some shifting!"

Captain Ashdown arrived behind me, as Vince sat and put his head in his hands.

"How many men per boat, lad?" the Captain asked the sailor.

"Fifteen, at most, sir," the young man replied. "Maybe ten per dinghy. Able Seaman Jones at your command, sir!"

"Good to meet you, Jones," said Captain Ashdown. "What about your vessel. Can it take four hundred or more men?"

"We're a passenger ship, sir," said Jones. "Eight hundred and twenty-two tonnes. It'll be a squeeze. And we've already taken fifty souls on board, sir!"

"Not a problem," the Captain told him. "Anything's better than sitting here, waiting to be killed."

"Yes, sir!"

As Jones' mates arrived, we began to organise the men. There were ten vessels in total, six boats and four dinghies, with a half hour round trip between the jetty and the Merchant Navy ship. The first wave took an age to send off and braved an ongoing air raid to get back to their goal. But once the boats returned empty, the second wave went much quicker, as we'd organised the groups in advance. In total, the boats made four trips, often under a substantial onslaught, and the whole process took nearly two and half hours.

I stayed on with Mush, Vince and Captain Ashdown. Captain Morrow had gone ahead to liaise with the ship's officers and smooth out any difficulties. I was impressed with Morrow's change of heart, and happy that he'd decided to help us. I thought of Sergeant Buckingham too, and despite our differences, hoped that he would make it safely home. My heart bled for Vince, however, and the loss of his giant friend. I could not imagine how it might feel to lose Mush.

When the final trip was ready, I called out to Vince, who had not moved, nor stopped hoping that Milligan would turn up. He sat alone, staring out to sea, lost in his own thoughts.

"You need to come with us," I told him. "I'm sorry, but Milligan is gone."

"But, he can't be," said a forlorn Vince. "We were going to have a pint together, meet up after things calmed down, meet each other's families. We've been through hell together, me and him."

"Please, friend!" I told him. "We have no time. They will leave without us."

He stared into my eyes.

"Vince!" I urged. "It is now or never! We must get going. If we lose this chance, we may not get another."

"You're right, Fazal," he said. "There's nothing to be done."

He edged from the platform, into the sea, and climbed aboard a rowing boat, with Mush right behind him. Several other men had joined us, having waded or swum out from the beach. Captain Ashdown took them all, and then he turned and shouted up to me. Only, I did not hear what he said. I only heard the hornets and I froze. The Stukas were returning from yet another raid on the docks, but they had plenty in reserve for us. For close to three hours, we had managed to evade their sorties and evacuate over four hundred men. Now, they would not fail.

Machine-gun fire erupted all around us, followed by a bomb to the rear that threw up more water. The last thing I saw was Captain Ashdown's horrified expression and Mush screaming as silently as the mules we had betrayed. Then I was falling again, blown clear from the makeshift jetty, but away from the now fast-receding boats. As I crashed under the water, I managed to right myself and swim for the surface. I told myself that I was safe underwater, but I was not. The bullets zipped past me, and I ducked under and swam towards the nearest vehicle.

I must have caught my head. I do not know, because I lost consciousness. . .

My grandfather laughed at me. He held out his hand, pulling me from the watering hole. The hornets buzzed all around us, a blanket of doom.

"I told you," he said. "When the hornets swarm, they will follow you until they are satisfied. Not even the water will save you. They will simply hover until you come up for air, or watch you drown. . ."

"But what can I do?" I pleaded. "How can I save myself?"

My grandfather held a half-eaten mango, succulent and ripe and dripping with juice. He threw it as far as he could, and one by one, the hornets chased after it, until they were all gone.

"There is always a way," he said.

Always a way. . .

I felt another hand, pulling me up and away. I screamed and kicked and tried to stay under.

"No!" I yelled. "The hornets are still waiting!"

A hefty slap stung my left cheek.

"COME ON!" a man shouted.

"He needs to be revived," a woman's voice added.

I felt sand against my back and pressure on my chest. Someone was pushing down with their hands, pumping and pumping, and then I tasted salt, as water and bile erupted from my mouth. I turned sideways, choking and spitting and trying to catch my breath.

"He's made it!" the woman said. "He'll live."

Another person knelt beside me.

"Private Khan!" she said. "It's me, Lillian."

I opened my eyes to see her smiling down at me.

"You're safe, Private," she told me. "You're back on the beach."

"B-but. . .!" I began, only for her to shush me.

"Calm down and try to breathe normally," she said. "You almost drowned out there."

"The boats!" I croaked. "Where are the boats?"

"They've gone," she replied. "You were blasted into the water and they left without you. Don't worry, we'll find you another boat, I'm sure."

I turned and looked out to sea, and my heart sank. The makeshift jetty remained, despite being battered in places, but the sea beyond lay empty. They were gone, all of them. Mush and Captain Ashdown, and Vince. They had left without me, perhaps convinced that I had drowned after the explosion. Unable to wait for one man, when the lives of so many might be put at risk. I understood their decision. It made sense. But it did not help me. I was lost, and back where I had started. Only this time, I had no one to support me. No one I could call upon. I was all alone.

"*NO!*" I groaned.

23

Back at the medical station in Malo-les-Bains, I was allowed to rest and regain my strength, what little remained of it. My uniform was dry and stiff with salt, and I was cut and bruised and sore. The sound of air raids and bombs remained a constant background, as the Germans continued to hamper the evacuation.

"We're running out of supplies," Lillian told me. "After tomorrow, we won't have anything left."

I was drinking tea and trying to gather my thoughts. I needed a new plan, another way to leave.

"Will you be evacuated then?" I asked her.

"I think so," she told me. "We're not much use without medical kits and morphine."

I nodded and sipped more tea.

"That's almost the last of the tea, too," she added. "And we've next to no food left. This effort is taking its toll, Fazal. I'm not sure what will happen now."

I shrugged.

"Nor me," I replied. "Without my Company, and the support of Captain Ashdown, I am lost."

"Why don't you make your way to the evacuation lines and join them?" she asked. "There are more boats now, and the troops are getting away."

"You know why," I reminded her. "We were to be left behind."

Lillian shook her head.

"No one will know or care," she said. "Go out and take a look, Private. It's absolute bedlam, with troops fending for themselves. Who will notice you in amongst all of that?"

I gave a wry smile.

"But I am not like the others," I told her. "My skin will stand out first. If they have heard the order, they will not let me board a ship."

Lillian disagreed.

"You'll be one man amongst hundreds," she told me. "And most good people will not deny you, Fazal. There is still decency and honour, even here in this hell."

"Perhaps," I replied.

"I'd take you with us," she added. "But we're strictly monitored and will have a military police escort. I'm not sure you'd pass for a nurse."

"Not even if I shaved and painted my face white?" I joked.

"Not even then," she said, not smiling.

I set down my cup and stood.

"I have taken too much of your time," I told her. "I will be on my way. Thank you for saving me."

"I did nothing," she replied. "Thank whoever dragged you from the water and the nurse who revived you."

"I would like to," I said, "but I do not see them around."

"Then, pray for their safe return, Private," said Lillian. "And try not to get blown up again."

I smiled.

"I was lucky," I replied. "Ten feet closer and the bomb would have left nothing of me. I'm simply pleased that my friends and comrades escaped."

"I wish you had too," she said. "Now, off you go, and let's hope we don't meet again."

I trudged away, back towards the beaches. It was the last time I would see Lillian.

I ambled around for what was left of the afternoon. Along the western perimeter, the lines were four men wide and snaked all the way back to the coastal road. They seemed to be heading for the concrete and wood jetty that stretched a mile into the sea. As I walked, I heard some of the men refer to it as the "Mole", although I was sure that was not its actual name. Whatever it was truly called, it had become the centre of attention, and I could see rescue ships in the deep water, edging closer to it.

Boredom and despondency caused me ill thoughts. I questioned the point of surviving my fall. Surely, I would have been better off drowning? At least, I would have gained some peace, rather than this waking nightmare of helplessness and dejection. But soon I realised that self-pity would not ease my burdens. There was absolutely no point in moping around. It would achieve nothing.

"You need a plan," I said to myself. "You need to think."

I no longer cared about my surroundings, nor whether others heard me talking to myself. There was no room for such things, and I was not alone in that. As I walked, I saw men relieving themselves in full view – digging latrines in the sand and then covering them over. I saw living men pulling the boots from the dead, even taking their socks and the contents of their packs. None of it mattered, not really, and what good were socks to a dead man anyway?

"We're no better than animals," one Tommy said in passing. "Not when things go awry."

I ignored him and continued on, aimless and apathetic. I had nowhere to go, and nothing to do, it seemed.

Wandering for hours until dusk fell left me sleepy and numb. I collapsed on the beach, very close to the long jetty. I had found a fire-damaged supply truck, and took shelter beside it, facing the town itself. The wind was stronger, but the raids had ceased, so I felt safe for a while. Not that safety mattered when survival was about luck not judgement. Two British men lay close by, and one of them nodded towards me.

"Hello," I said.

The man nodded again before closing his eyes. I settled with my back to a wheel and tried to get some rest. However, sleep only lasted so long. I would doze until I heard loud voices, or some other noise, then awaken once more. Then I'd be off again, until my head lolled sideways, and I awoke with a start. Eventually, I lay on the damp sand, using my jacket as a sheet. That left me cold but allowed a couple of hours of uninterrupted slumber.

By dawn, I was on my feet. I plodded down to the water and washed my face, hoping to feel refreshed. But the salt water only reminded me of my near-drowning and of my failed escape, and I grew gloomy again. My stomach growled with hunger, a tiger without prey, and began to ache. My head was light, my legs cramped, and I was foot-sore. I needed food and water, so I headed for the road, hoping to scavenge something in amongst the broken buildings.

An hour of searching passed before I came across the dead soldier. He was lying under a pile of rubble, and at first, I only saw his boots. Initially, I intended to afford him some dignity, but as I removed the rubble, I saw his pack and the chocolate bars within. A cantina of water sat next to his shattered legs, and I picked it up and found it half-full. I took them without hesitation and tried not to think too much about the morality of my situation. Leaving him uncovered, so that he might be discovered, I moved on quickly, filling my belly and quenching my thirst.

Finally, I headed back to the beach, eager to see what was happening. The skies had cleared, and the sun was shining, and my heart sank again. Perfect conditions meant we were easier targets for the Germans, and so it proved, as they began another day of relentless raids. I sat down beside some abandoned supply boxes and put my head in my hands. I had no choice but to join the lines of men and pray that no one objected to my presence. However, I did not get up and do that. Instead I sat and wondered how my life had reached such a point. And I cursed the day I had decided to run away and join up.

24

I eventually reached the Mole during mid-afternoon. More precisely, I reached the end of the queue. A line, four men wide, stretched out before me. And on the jetty, they stood four abreast too, held back about fifty metres along. There, they climbed down onto smaller boats, or swam for it, trying to reach the larger vessels beyond.

I joined in, keeping my head down, and edging forward with the crowd. Most of the men paid me no mind, and we made steady progress for an hour, despite the air raids. It's hard to explain the constant threat of the planes vividly enough. Imagine being so worn out, so disoriented, that you stand in the open watching on, as death wails and caterwauls towards you like some demonic banshee, and you do not even flinch. For some men, the resignation went beyond even that.

"If you're going to kill us," shouted one drained Tommy, "just get on with it. I'm tired of this!"

Suddenly, the men began to cheer. When I looked to see what the fuss was about, my heart leapt in hope. A fleet of boats appeared in convoy, perhaps twenty in total, ranging from three huge destroyers to smaller vessels that seemed like toy ships in comparison. On the jetty, much further out past the troops, I saw some movement and wondered what was going on.

"It's happening, lads!" someone shouted behind me.

"We're going home!" yelled another, causing me to think of Milligan the day before.

Within the hour, the situation changed again. The troops were ordered to move along the Mole, right down to the far end. The lines moved at a pace, and about a half-mile away, I watched the ships pull alongside the jetty, and span the gap with ladders and planks. Soon, a stream of troops was boarding at a terrific pace. And above us, on a lookout tower, a senior officer spoke into a loudhailer, organising everything from on high. My spirits soared, and I dared to think about reaching the safety of England again. My only fear was the Germans. From their positions, and through their sorties, news would spread of this new evacuation tactic. It would not be long before they attacked the Mole.

I turned eastwards, expecting to see the planes zeroing in, but instead I saw clear skies. On the beaches of Malo-les-Bains and further along, thousands of men were still wading out to sea, trying to reach a flotilla of rowing boats. And behind me, Dunkirk continued to burn and smoulder, and I wondered where Lillian had gone, and whether she was safe. I watched the scenes to the east for some time, being jostled along, until someone shouted at me.

"You!" I heard.

Someone poked me in the arm.

"You, Private!"

I turned to see a tall and senior British officer glaring at me. He pointed to the Mole.

"Combat troops first," he told me. "We've no space for service corps yet!"

I shook my head.

"I'm very sorry, sir," I replied. "I'm Private Khan of Company 32, RIASC. My officer, John Ashdown and the rest of my company were evacuated yesterday. We were attacked, and I fell into the sea. I was left behind."

The officer sneered.

"I don't care if you're the king of Hindustan itself!" he roared. "You have no right to take the place of a Tommy!"

"But I must get to England and find my company," I protested.

"Not before a single Englishman!" the officer

replied. "Besides, your orders were to wait behind, if I'm not mistaken. What was the name of your officer again?"

I felt sick. My stomach turned, and my mouth grew even drier. Not one of my fellow comrades intervened on my behalf. Not one protested at the immorality of pushing me aside, when I was as much a part of the effort as everyone else. I was in trouble, and so was Captain Ashdown. I decided to play dumb.

"I'm sorry," I said. "I must be mistaken. I will leave now."

"You will not—" began the officer, only to be shoved aside by a sudden surge of men.

The Germans were back, and they had come in numbers. As the familiar sounds of whining engines, exploding bombs and strafing bullets resumed, I took the opportunity to escape. Going against the crowd was impossible, so I edged to my left, and out of the line. Then, with my head low, I jogged back towards the town. I only stopped when I had put some distance between myself and the jetty. Finally, I collapsed by a pile of rubble and cursed my luck.

I stayed there for some time as darkness fell, shrouded in self-pity once more. I knew I needed to act but doubt and despair prevented it. Sitting back, I thought of all I had endured until that point, of the cruelty and barbarism I had witnessed. The faith and optimism that had been torn from me, only to be returned in increments then dashed again. What was the point?

Down by the beach, I saw torchlights flashing out into the shallows. Despite the darkness, those men continued to move forward, continued to have hope. Giving up was not an option, and as my grandfather had said in my dream – there is always a way. I stood and headed down to them, careful not to allow myself any confidence. Not yet. As the water lapped against my worn boots, I watched perhaps fifty men call out into the night.

"SOS!" they called. "Is anyone there?"

Another Tommy brushed past, and then another. The third one apologised.

"Sorry mate," he said, and my mouth fell open.

"Private Smith?" I said in astonishment.

Sid Smith stopped and turned, then shone a torch in my face.

"Blinkin' hell!" he said. "Private Khan. Why are you wandering about in the darkness?"

I could not contain my smile.

"My company have been evacuated," I explained. "We got attacked and I was thrown into the water. They left without me."

Sid nodded. "So, you're on your own?"

"Yes," I replied. "And Command has ordered that Indians be left behind."

Sid grimaced.

"No surprise," he replied. "Stupid, useless bunch of buffoons!"

"So, I am in a pickle, as you English say."

"No, Khan," said Sid. "You're not. You're coming with us."

"But I—"

Sid grabbed my arm.

"There's fifteen of us —all from various units. We've been told to get back by any means possible. We've no officers, no posh boys to tell us what to do. You're more than welcome."

I began to dream again, but immediately reality kicked my aspiration in the guts.

"They will not let me board," I told him. "Because I am Indian."

"*Really?*" said Sid. "I'd like to see them try. Once you're out there, Khan, they won't stop you. Not if you're with us."

"Perhaps," I replied.

"So," Sid added, "you coming or not?"

I did not have to consider his offer for very long.

"If you will have me, friend," I told him, "then I

am honoured to accept."

"Stuff honour," said Private Smith. "That nonsense just gets you killed. Come on!"

25

We waded out until the water was at our shoulders. Sid kept his arms aloft the entire time, flashing his torch on and off. We must have stood like that for forty minutes or longer, but none of the rowing boats were drawn to us. Yet, we were not deterred. Other men *were* being rescued, and we would simply have to wait our turn.

"The batteries will die before they come," Sid complained.

"If your arms are tired," I said through chattering teeth, "I could hold the torch instead?"

The water was cold and briny, and occasionally a surge would cause it to enter our mouths. I ended up with seaweed and other stuff in my hair and on my face. A light mist had settled over us, too, and it made things more difficult.

"Wait!" said Sid.

He turned his torch to full beam. I heard splashes,

perhaps thirty yards away. And then saw three flashes of light.

"Over here!" Sid yelled. "This way!"

He grinned at me.

"Yes!" he said. "This is it, Khan!"

A white dinghy appeared, steered by a lone rower.

"Are you there?" he called out.

"Here!" Sid and I shouted in unison. "We're here!"

The man turned his light towards us and we were momentarily blinded.

"I've got you," he shouted back. "Hang on!"

Sid looked at me with a grimace.

"*Hang on?*" he said. "What does he think we've been doing?"

Sid babbled on, perhaps overwhelmed at the thought of being rescued. I was not so positive. After my two previous experiences, I held my emotions in check. This time, I would wait until we reached English soil before truly believing again.

The dinghy seemed to take an age to reach us, but once it did, the man was only too pleased to help us aboard. However, he was very young and dressed in civilian clothes, and not what we had expected.

"Hello lads!" he said. "Connor Bridges at your service."

"Private Khan," I replied. "Delighted to meet you."

"Sid from Tooting," said Private Smith. "It's cold!"

Connor grinned.

"Glad to see your sense of humour ain't failed," he told Sid.

"You don't look like Navy," Sid replied. "Where's your uniform?"

The young man removed his cloth cap and chuckled.

"Ain't got one," he said. "I'm a fisherman, from Margate."

"So, what the hell are you doing here?" asked Sid. He looked amazed.

Connor shrugged.

"My dad heard they needed boats for the evacuation, so we came to help," he explained. "There's me, Dad and my Uncle Pat. We've done one trip already. Thought we'd try again."

"You're evacuating men?" I said. "As *civilians*?"

He looked at me and nodded.

"You ain't the same as 'im," he said, nodding towards Sid. "Where you from then?"

"India," I replied. "My unit evacuated the day before yesterday and I was left behind."

"India?"

"Yes," I told him.

"Blimey," he said. "There's a Hindu gentleman does palm readings on the pier, but I've never spoken to him. You're the first proper Indian I've ever met. You a soldier?"

"No," I said. "I'm with the Royal Indian Army Service Corps."

"Oh right," the lad said. "Like, helpin' out?"

"Something like that," said Sid. "How big is your old man's boat?"

"Big enough," said Connor, with a certain pride. "We took fifteen blokes back earlier. It was a bit tight, but we made it."

"That'll do us!" Sid told him. "How many more men you taking?"

"I can take a few more," Connor told us. "But not many."

He rowed on, rescuing five more men from the water, and then he turned around.

"This dinghy is for six," he explained. "I can't risk it."

"How long to the boat?" asked Sid.

"Fifteen minutes at most," said Connor. "We're just off the shallows."

"And how many men on board already?" Sid added.

"Dunno," he said. "Depends on how many Uncle Pat finds."

He checked a small compass by torchlight, before steering the dinghy in the right direction. Sid and another soldier lit the way using their torches. Time slowed yet again, but without the threat of German planes I was far more relaxed. Eventually, we closed in on the fishing boat. It was tiny and crammed with men and was battered and worn. Connor's father helped us aboard before giving me a funny look. He was a big man and reminded me of Milligan. His face was weathered, and his left hand was missing its little finger.

"You one of ours?" he asked in a gruff voice.

"He is," Sid said on my behalf. "Indian Corps. Why, is that a problem?"

Connor's dad shook his head.

"No, friend," he said. "Just wondered. I'm Danny Bridges. Pleased to have you aboard."

He pointed at his brother.

"That's Pat," he told us. "He's got jumpers and blankets, and tea somewhere. Might be a few biscuits too. We're setting off now, so we should be in Dover soon enough."

I looked up at him.

"Thank you for your kindness," I said.

"It's no bother," Danny replied. "It's my duty, Private. Hold tight though, the sea's a bit choppy tonight."

Sid and I sat together on the tiny crowded deck, as the little boat bobbed along, taking us to safety. The other rescued men sat close by, and we shared a few jokes. No one pointed out my ethnic origin, nor cared that I was service corps and not combat ready. We were all one, shattered and thirsty, relieved and hungry, heading to the English mainland.

In the end, the short journey was uneventful, almost serene, which was both welcome and surprising considering what had gone before. We had been through hell together, all of us with stories to tell, yet I wondered whether mine would be heard.

I had begun my journey with high hopes and naïve ideas of honour and duty. Dreams of following in my beloved Baba's footsteps, earning glory through service, and experiencing the camaraderie and loyalty of military life. The child in me had even yearned for medals and perhaps a touch of recognition.

But my time in France had put paid to that innocence. For the first time, I had learned of my place in the pecking order of British India. I was one place above my unfortunate mules. Almost as bestial in the eyes of my supposed masters, almost as expendable. Almost as voiceless.

Yet, as we said goodbye to Connor and his family, and disembarked at Dover's Eastern Pier, I was not once deemed an outsider, nor lower than my peers. I was treated with compassion and warmth by the Bridges, and then the ordinary folk of the town, and given my share of sandwiches and tea. This reception warmed my heart, and something dawned on me. Everyday people like Connor and his family, and those in Dover, were no different to me, nor the regular soldiers with whom I shared the journey '*home*'. We were the cannon fodder that Sid had spoken of on our first meeting. Lillian's pawns, being shunted around a board with no thought for our lives. Above us, on a social hierarchy they had created, sat senior officers and politicians, kings and emperors. They made the orders and we were expected to follow. The colour of our faces, the gods to whom we bowed, the food we ate or did not eat – none of that meant anything. We were the same.

Later, Sid and I, separated from our own units, watched as those in regiments marched off together towards Dover Marine train station.

"Not for me," he said as he watched them leave. "I'm done with this hell."

"You will not return to your regiment?" I asked.

"Probably," he said after some thought. "But only because they'll court martial me if I don't. Besides, after the fiasco we've just experienced, they'll be enlisting men, never mind allowing them to decommission."

"So, what will you do?" I asked.

"Who knows, friend?" he replied. "Right now, I

want a pint of ale, a bath and a bed."

We sat a while longer, just watching the world go by. The sense of tranquillity and lack of danger was as welcome as it was unusual. A group of young women stopped when they saw us, handing out packets of cigarettes, chocolate and more sandwiches. Sid engaged in idle chat with them, grinning at me every few moments. Then an older woman appeared, pushing a small, two-wheeled cart. She opened it and took out two bottles.

"It's only mild," she told us, "but you look like you could use it."

I began to tell her that I didn't drink, but Sid elbowed me in the ribs.

"What my Indian brother means," said Sid, "is that he can't drink it now. He's got a train to catch."

"Oh, rest a while," said the woman. "The bleedin' army can wait."

Sid took both bottles, putting one aside, and opening the other by holding it against the metal edge of a wooden box and pushing down with some force. The ale gushed out in an eruption of light brown froth. He placed the bottle to his lips and drank quickly.

"I needed that," he said, blowing out his cheeks and belching. "You want some?"

"I cannot," I reminded him.

"You sure?" he said, pretending to look around. "No one's watching."

I looked at the bottle and thought of Baba and the stories he'd told me. The things he had seen and done that would scandalise our neighbours. But I was my own man now, and I did not want to drink.

"I'm sure," I said.

We heard footsteps approaching, alongside a tapping sound. A senior officer, walking with a cane, despite having no limp. He carried a clipboard in his other hand.

"What are you chaps doing?" he asked.

Sid smiled.

"Not dying, sir," he replied. "Despite the government's best efforts."

The officer raised an eyebrow.

"I'll let that go for today, Private," he replied. "But only once. You need to get yourselves to Dover Marine and find trains to your barracks."

I shook my head.

"But I do not know where my company went, sir," I said. "I was separated from them."

The officer nodded.

"RIASC?" he said.

"Yes, sir." He checked his records, flipping through a few sheets.

"Company 32, under Captain John Ashdown," he told me. "Aldershot barracks."

He turned to Sid.

"What about you, Private?"

Sid grinned.

"Don't worry about it, me old mucker," he said. "I know exactly where I'm going."

The officer shrugged and walked away, *tap-tap-tapping* his cane.

"Where will you go?" I asked.

"Oh, I reckon they can wait," said Sid. "I'm off home to see me old mother. Why don't you come along?"

I shook my head and thought of seeing Mush once again.

"I cannot," I told him. "*Hukum Hai.*"

At Dover Marine, Sid's train to London arrived first. He turned and held out his hand.

"Been a pleasure, Fazal," he said.

I took his hand and placed my other on his shoulder.

"I owe you a debt of gratitude," I told him. "It will remain with me until I die."

"Well," said Sid, "if you're ever in Tooting Broadway, look me up. Sidney Smith of Himley Road. Everyone knows me."

I nodded.

"And, if you're ever in Rawalpindi..." I began.

"Oh, behave yourself, mate!" he joked, before growing serious. "Take care, Fazal. You've been a good friend."

"You too, Sid," I replied. "I would not be here without you."

My train arrived ten minutes later and was packed to the rafters. I found a spot beside some engineers who were drunk and boisterous, and having lots of fun. And, as the train chugged away from Dover, I closed my eyes and dreamt of home.

EPILOGUE

March 1944

I had run away before dawn, and I returned at the same time. The lane was silent, the carriage driver I'd hired in Rawalpindi having departed. A stray dog foraged amongst some bushes and I heard the reassuring buzz of insects. The sound of home. It was warm and humid, a welcome relief after years of dull and cold weather.

At the gates of my family home, I hesitated. I was unsure of the welcome that awaited, and whether it would be a welcome at all. Perhaps my years away had hardened my parents against me. Perhaps their anger would override their relief at finding out that I had survived. I had considered writing to them many, many times since Dunkirk, yet had not done so once. I don't know if the cause was shame or pride, but something prevented it.

After saying goodbye to Sid Smith, I re-joined

Company 32 in Aldershot, before we were sent north to a place called Ashbourne in Derbyshire. We stayed for many months, Mush and I, even enjoying a visit from King George VI and Queen Elizabeth, before moving on again. We next found ourselves in Brecon, Wales, with new animals and new tasks. The new mules retained their voice boxes, and often their braying became grating. Each time one of them cried out, I thought of my silent comrades and how they had been left behind.

Not once did we return to the battlefront, even though we trained just in case the order came. It was a relief after France, but soon the calm and the endless repetition of duties made me homesick. I had come to Europe to find glory, not to become a glorified herder of animals.

Then Mush fell ill with pneumonia and died. In my backpack was a grainy photograph, taken and developed for me by a kind local newspaperman. It showed nine grey headstones, each inscribed in Urdu and English, set against a darker grey wall and surrounded by snow-flecked grass. The one to the forefront read "Mushtaq Ahmed" and gave details of his service and the date of his passing – October 19th, 1942. I vowed to deliver it to Mush's family, should I ever make it back to India.

The rest of my time in Britain passed through

a haze of duty, training exercises and many tears. Captain Ashdown was gone, having been disciplined for breaking the order at Dunkirk. Mush was gone too, his dreams of a better life for his family dashed in the cruellest of circumstances. Imagine surviving the hell of Dunkirk, only to be undone by wet and cold weather in a strange country so far from home? Each time I thought of my dear friend, my heart broke.

Finally, in January 1944, what was left of Force K6 was disbanded and ordered back to India. I was eager to leave, despite having met many wonderful British people. My thoughts turned back to my own country, and to my family. I had embarked on a great adventure but learned many harsh and soul-destroying lessons. I did not find the glory I craved. I did not feel that I had followed in Baba's footsteps. My nightmares were filled with senseless and brutal deaths, and the horrors of Dunkirk. Mostly they involved the incessant and pitiless droning of those Stukas.

I heard a lock being undone, a latch being lifted. As the tall wooden gates swung open, my heart thumped inside my chest and my stomach churned. My parents stood before me, weeping, their faces showing only relief.

"You have come home, son," said my mother, holding out her hand.

I took it and nodded.

"Yes, Mother," I replied. "I am home now. It was my duty to return. *Hukum Hai.*"

My mother nodded and led me inside, as my father closed the gates behind me.

AUTHOR NOTE

In 2005, I began to research the role of Indian soldiers during both world wars. Being of Indian heritage, I knew that India had participated, but I was shocked to discover the true extent of that role. That early research resulted in a novel called *City of Ghosts*, published in 2009. But my interest in the role of India in the world wars did not end there. The more I read, the more I discovered, the more frustrated I became.

Born and schooled in England, I wanted to know why I had never been taught about the brave service of so-called "empire soldiers" – from India, the Caribbean, Africa and many other places. Where were the memorials, the plaques, the photographs and the film footage? More importantly, where was mention of these brave men and women when Remembrance Day came each year?

The British Armed Forces have always remembered

and celebrated the role of non-white personnel. The Imperial War Museum, in particular, took a lead in highlighting the roles of these people. However, there was little shown in the media and even resistance from some people who claimed that the role of non-white troops was overblown, a result of "political correctness", and in some cases, made up.

Fast forward to 2017, when the film *Dunkirk* released, and a furore began. Some argued that the film ignored the role of non-white service personnel. Others claimed that there weren't any non-white participants. The latter is entirely untrue. There were many non-white personnel at Dunkirk – specifically members of the Royal Indian Army Service Corps (RIASC). These predominantly Muslim personnel were mule corps, or muleteers, responsible for supplying the lines and transporting resources across France during the vicious winter of 1939 into 1940. They performed a difficult and vital task, whilst many thousands of miles from home, for an Empire that had taken their lands and their rights. Then, in May 1940, they were sent to Dunkirk – only to be betrayed.

One man, their British officer, ignored a shameful order to leave non-military personnel behind at Dunkirk. His name was Captain John Ashdown (father of British politician, Paddy Ashdown) and alongside his muleteers, he is an unsung hero of World War Two. Fluent in Urdu and Punjabi and with a deep love for India, John ensured that his personnel were evacuated. He was court-martialled for his brave and honourable actions – although that ruling was later rescinded – and his heroic service has remained widely unknown. I hope that my story will help to change that and am grateful to John's son Mark Ashdown for providing greater detail about his father.

What of the muleteers after Dunkirk? Well, most were initially stationed in Derbyshire, where the King and Queen paid them a visit. From there, they were sent to various parts of the UK, and most did not take part in military action again. Sadly, some died, and were buried in cemeteries across Wales and Scotland, in particular. You can still visit their headstones today. All in all, approximately one thousand non-white personnel were evacuated from Dunkirk, although their mules were not so fortunate.

The story of Captain John Ashdown, the RIASC and their mules, and their part in Dunkirk needs to be told. I am proud to have told that tale, and hope that you have enjoyed it. Perhaps you will learn a little more about this hidden aspect of British history, too.

Bali Rai, 2018

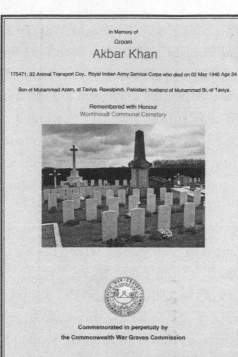

In Memory of
Groom
Akbar Khan

175471, 32 Animal Transport Coy., Royal Indian Army Service Corps who died on 02 May 1940 Age 24

Son of Muhammad Azam, of Taviya, Rawalpindi, Pakistan; husband of Muhammad Bi, of Taviya.

Remembered with Honour
Wormhoudt Communal Cemetery

Commemorated in perpetuity by
the Commonwealth War Graves Commission

Akbar Khan, the only Company 32 casualty during the retreat from Dunkirk.

Reproduced courtesy of the Commonwealth War Graves Commission.

Captain John Ashdown in formal uniform.

Photograph of John Ashdown reproduced courtesy of the Ashdown family.

204